ONLY THE BEGINNING . . .

Even standing perfectly still, Acephelos dripped menace. There was an air of deadly intent about the demon that none of the other things they had encountered so far came anywhere near matching. It wasn't just that he could take your head: it was something that made it clear killing you would only be the beginning of the things he would do.

The Legend of Sleepy Hollow struck fear with his mere presence.

The Horseman paused and turned slightly in the saddle, the saber in his gloved hand pointing up toward the bloated moon and the scattered clouds.

Then he looked at them.

He had no head, he had no eyes, but he looked at them. And Aimee was sure that he recognized them.

THE HOLLOW

BOOK ONE: HORSEMAN

BOOK TWO: DROWNED

BOOK THREE: MISCHIEF

BOOK FOUR: ENEMIES

THE HOLLOW

BOOK FOUR:
ENEMIES

BY
CHRISTOPHER GOLDEN
&
FORD LYTLE GILMORE

razor
bill

The Hollow 4: Enemies

RAZORBILL

Published by the Penguin Group
Penguin Young Readers Group
345 Hudson Street, New York, New York 10014, U.S.A.
Penguin Group (USA) Inc., 375 Hudson Street, New York, New York 10014,
U.S.A.
Penguin Group (Canada), 90 Eglinton Avenue, Suite 700, Toronto,
Ontario, Canada M4P 2Y3 (a division of Pearson Penguin Canada Inc.)
Penguin Books Ltd, 80 Strand, London WC2R 0RL, England
Penguin Ireland, 25 St Stephen's Green, Dublin 2, Ireland
(a division of Penguin Books Ltd)
Penguin Group (Australia), 250 Camberwell Road, Camberwell,
Victoria 3124, Australia (a division of Pearson Australia Group Pty Ltd)
Penguin Books India Pvt Ltd, 11 Community Centre, Panchsheel Park,
New Delhi – 110 017, India
Penguin Group (NZ), Cnr Airborne and Rosedale Roads, Albany,
Auckland 1310, New Zealand (a division of Pearson New Zealand Ltd)
Penguin Books (South Africa) (Pty) Ltd, 24 Sturdee Avenue, Rosebank,
Johannesburg 2196, South Africa

Penguin Books Ltd, Registered Offices: 80 Strand, London WC2R 0RL,
England

10 9 8 7 6 5 4 3 2 1

Copyright 2006 © Christopher Golden and Ford Lytle Gilmore
All rights reserved

Interior design by Christopher Grassi

Library of Congress Cataloging-in-Publication Data

Printed in the United States of America

For Bonnie Moore.
—C. G.

For my muse, Larissa Miller.
—F. L. G.

AUTHORS' NOTE

Local historians in various towns, most of them in Westchester County, New York, have argued for ages about what town or village was author Washington Irving's inspiration for the hamlet featured in his famous story "The Legend of Sleepy Hollow." For years, North Tarrytown, New York, stood firm in its claim to be the main influence on the creation of that fictional town. In 1996, the village officially changed its name to Sleepy Hollow. If you visit Sleepy Hollow now, you'll see signs everywhere promoting the name and the image of the Headless Horseman, a boon to tourism. Despite the horror of the original tale, there seems something charming about the legend.

For the moment.

Meanwhile, readers who are familiar with Sleepy Hollow, New York (where Golden lived for three years in the early nineties), will notice that while some familiar landmarks are included, many liberties have been taken with the geography of the place.

We won't tell if you won't.

ENEMIES

CHAPTER ONE

HALLOWEEN IN SLEEPY Hollow was different from Halloween in the rest of the world. The tourists came to town like it was Christmas and they'd just gotten off the Polar Express. Main Street had been transformed by the holiday. The long, sloping road was littered with people milling around, looking through the street carnival's various tents and stands. The scent of fresh kettle corn drifted through the air, mingling with aromas from the sandwich shop offering wedges and the half-dozen cafés that dealt in decent food and coffee at exorbitant prices.

Someone was playing a grainy-sounding mix of creepy Halloween music through an old CD player, and the music gave Aimee Lancaster pleasant little chills. It seemed like half of the town had turned out for the last day of the Harvest Festival. At the station at the bottom of the hill, on the bank of the Hudson River, commuter trains disgorged people who were getting home from work in Manhattan.

The trains pulled in every half hour or so, spilling out forty or fifty people at a time, most of whom looked like they were in a hurry. Halloween was a night for kids, and their parents didn't want to keep them waiting.

The street was already overrun with kids, little ones, dressed as ghosts and comic book heroes, cowboys and princesses, and just about everything in between. A toddler walked past the spot where Aimee, her brother, Shane, and her best friend, Stasia, waited for the rest of their group. The little boy was dressed as SpongeBob SquarePants and was holding on to his mommy's hand for dear life.

There were almost as many older kids in costumes, even some people around Aimee's age. For the tykes there was a costume contest with prizes that was supposed to start soon. For Aimee and her friends there would be a costume party in a few hours, and it was a good excuse to be someone else for a while. That was almost always a good thing.

From far above her head Aimee heard a soft "boo," just as massive hands blocked her eyes without actually touching her face.

Aimee smiled. There was only one person she knew big enough to match those hands. She turned around and stared at a massive wall covered in black cloth. When she took a step back, the wall resolved into Mark Hyde, the biggest person she'd ever met.

Hyde wasn't fat—he was just very, very tall and very broad.

Jekyll was with him, as usual. Steve Delisle was the smartest kid in their class, and a lot of kids thought it was strange that he'd chosen a bruiser and former bully like Hyde as his best friend. The skinny little brain ought to have been able to predict people nicknaming him Dr. Jekyll, but it never seemed to bother him.

In fact, the two of them obviously liked the Jekyll-and-Hyde comparison well enough, because for Halloween, they'd dressed as themselves. Or at least as their literary counterparts. Mark was dressed in an old-fashioned suit with a cloak, a top hat, and a walking stick with a brass head. He had also avoided shaving for most of the last week, and the resulting scruffy beard made him look bestial. His normally broad, handsome face had taken on a darker edge. Add one set of cheap plastic teeth and he was looking positively menacing. Jekyll was dressed in a decent brown suit that looked like it had come straight out of a movie about Victorian London and had thrown on a lab coat over it. He was wearing his glasses for a change and looked like he should have been living in another era.

To those who knew them, the costumes were just perfect.

Stasia and Shane both laughed at the sight of them.

"Oh my God!" Aimee said. "You guys look awesome!"

"You're looking pretty spectacular yourself, Miss Kitty." Jekyll chuckled as he spoke and used a very, very bad British accent.

Aimee smiled. She had chosen her cat costume for maximum impact.

Hyde gave Jekyll a light bump. "Steve, you know she always looks good."

Aimee's eyebrows raised in surprise. Hyde was pretty quiet in general and not known for spontaneous hit-and-run complimenting. Aimee wasn't sure quite how to respond. She gave him a little smile, unsure why she felt so shy all of a sudden.

Shane saved her by snapping a picture with his digital camera, half blinding them with the flash. He was taking a lot of pictures, probably to hide the fact that he felt stupid in his costume. He was dressed as a priest, complete with a large crucifix and a heavy black Bible. Her brother wasn't exactly comfortable in the outfit, but it worked well with Stasia's costume. She was dressed in a red vinyl suit that was practically painted on and had added a tail and large horns. Stasia had even gone all out and dyed her hair a flaming red.

And in contrast there was Aimee herself. She

was wearing a set of cat ears and was sporting a little black nose and whiskers courtesy of Stasia and a mascara pen.

Jekyll looked at her and purred loudly as he moved closer. "Want to figure out which of my pockets has the catnip in it, kitty?"

"Want to figure out where I'm hiding my can of pepper spray, Doc?"

"You wound me, my dear. I'm a doctor. I just wanted to make sure you take your medicine and offer you a free examination."

Jekyll's comment left her flustered again. He broke all the rules. He was supposed to be a complete stoner geek, and when he actually flirted, it was like something went wrong with the wiring in her head.

Though it wasn't the same as with Hyde. Mark was so often lost somewhere in his own head, his gaze distant, but tonight he seemed to be sort of focusing on her. It made Aimee feel self-conscious, but oddly enough, it also felt kind of good.

She shook off the attentions of both of her friends. It was Halloween night, and after all the real supernatural nasties they'd dealt with in the past couple of months, it was nice to be able to fall back into the routine of the faux spookiness of the holiday. Aimee intended to have some fun tonight, just relax and hang out with her friends.

Ever since the Capitol Theatre had finally reopened, it seemed like every night either Aimee was working or Stasia was. Sometimes both of them. Ella had reluctantly consented to let them both have Halloween night off, mainly because they whined a lot. Well, not that much, but Ella had realized how hard they were working and agreed to set them free for Halloween. There were enough other employees. If just barely.

Aimee glanced around, happy to be with this group of friends. What with the tensions that had developed a couple of weeks earlier and work and school, they hadn't really been together like this in a while. It was nice.

Hyde tapped Shane lightly on the shoulder. "How's the arm feeling?"

Shane rubbed his shoulder. "Like some damned gorilla punched me there harder than he meant to."

"I told you not to move. You didn't listen." Hyde smiled broadly. "You gotta listen when I say stuff like that."

"I'm getting that."

Jekyll pushed his glasses up his face and put an arm on each of the other guys' shoulders. "I'm still not seeing the wisdom of this. I told you I could teach you a little self-defense, Shane."

Hyde shook his head and snorted. "Maybe he'd like to learn this year."

"What do you mean by that?"

Jekyll was doing his best to sound offended, but no one was falling for it. With everything that they'd gone through in recent months, Shane had decided to actually learn a few things about defending himself. He'd never been a fighter. And obviously, if he was looking for a friend who could help in that department, Hyde would be the one.

Aimee could attest to that, just from looking at the size of him and having seen him fight. . . .

Aimee frowned. Her brain was suddenly so stuck on Hyde, and she couldn't figure it out. He was a quiet guy, with a dark streak in him. Not her type at all. Nope. She was definitely not falling for Mark Hyde.

Definitely not.

So why did she keep thinking about him?

Shane and the guys were clustered together now, talking about Shane's self-defense training. Stasia hip-checked Aimee. "You're gonna burn holes in his coat."

Her best friend's voice was teasing, with that same sultry quality it always had, just like Stasia herself. Dressed in the devil getup, Stasia was already drawing the eyes of most of the guys in the area, though Aimee was pleased to note a few of the people around them actually looking at her.

Aimee shot a withering glance at her. "What's that mean?"

Stasia glanced quickly over at the boys to make sure they were still out of earshot. She kept her voice low.

"I mean you keep looking that hard at Mark and you're gonna let the world know about your x-ray vision." Stasia leaned in closer, her eyes wrinkled with laugh lines in the gathering darkness. "When did you officially decide he was hot?"

Aimee felt her skin flush. "I didn't!"

"You were just checking out his butt." Stasia smiled, her lips playing between a smirk and a full grin. "I saw you, girl. You were looking at him like he was a prime cut of meat."

Stasia turned and looked Hyde over. She took her time assessing every feature. "You can't see much past that coat of his, but he's definitely got it going. Crazy hair, week's worth of beard, and all."

"I wasn't checking him out."

Stasia shrugged, her face perfectly deadpan. "You say so. Hell, he's worth looking at in my book."

"He's just not my type."

"Uh-huh. And you have so much experience, you've figured out what your *type* is supposed to be?" Stasia got that *oh, puh-LEASE* look on her face and blew air from between her lips in a half laugh. "Mark is *hot*. And he's dangerous. There're a lot of girls out there who like that combination."

"I'm not one of them," Aimee said, but the

moment the words were out, she knew it was a lie. And she knew Stasia knew it too.

Stasia wasn't going to let it go. "Yep. It'd be kind of like petting a big old lion. You know it's dangerous, but it feels so good running your fingers through that fur. . . ."

Even when she was being a pain in the ass, Stasia was good at putting Aimee at ease. Most of the girls at school seemed to have some kind of agenda. Stasia never did.

"I can't get him out of my head," Aimee confessed. "And he's not that dangerous. At least, not to his friends."

She looked at Hyde. He, Shane, and Jekyll were watching a small crowd across the street, a bunch of girls from the cheerleading squad. Kimmie Hill was with them, and Aimee saw that she was doing her very best to avoid noticing Shane. Aimee also noticed the way Hyde watched Kimmie.

Dressed in a Little Bo Peep outfit, Kimmie looked miserable. She'd dated Shane for all of two weeks before her brother broke it off with her. Aimee had no clue what he'd been thinking. She still wanted to kick him in the head for that but had decided he had to make his own choices.

The weird part was that Kimmie still seemed hung up on Shane. Mark would have done just about anything to have Kimmie as his girlfriend,

Aimee suspected, and the cheerleader never even noticed him.

That was part of the problem too. She didn't want to fall for Hyde when he was so obviously fixated on Kimmie.

Stasia narrowed her eyes, seeming to guess Aimee's thoughts. The girl was almost psychic when it came to reading the body language between people, the things they didn't say.

"You're never gonna know if Hyde could be that into you if you don't take a chance."

Aimee shook her head as though blowing off the comment, but the logic wasn't lost on her. When she looked back toward the guys, Hyde was tearing his gaze away from where Kimmie stood, his eyes hidden by shadows and the rest of his face tense and stony.

He had a rep as a bully, and for a long time he'd wanted people to think that was exactly what he was. Now that was all starting to change. All he wanted was a life where nobody pushed him into being something else.

Jekyll looked back over his shoulder at the girls. "What are you two conspiring about back there? If you want to seduce me, all you have to do is ask."

"Oh, honey, I wouldn't even have to ask," Stasia said. "I could finish you off with a look."

Steve Delisle was a funny guy, charming, but by

no means a ladies' man. Stasia's tone alone flustered him, never mind the tempting expression on her face. She did tempting way too well. He laughed at himself as he turned away.

"So," Stasia said. "Come on, Aimee, give me the reasons why you should stay away from Hyde."

Aimee thought about it. "Well, he's my brother's friend. That can't be a good thing."

"Why not?" Stasia gave her a funny look, one that Aimee couldn't read.

"What if we try and it doesn't work out? Where does that leave Shane?"

"With a sister and a friend who might not like to hang out. But that's not a good reason. Any relationship between you and Hyde is between you and Hyde. Shane's a big boy. If he has a problem with you two dating, he'll get over it."

"Just like that?" Aimee didn't really agree. Back when they were living in Boston, Shane had hooked up with one of her friends, and things had been really awkward afterward. Aimee had given him hell for that.

Stasia shrugged it off. "Yeah. Just like that. You'd still be his sister and Mark would still be his friend. What's life without a few risks? You see what you want, you should go for it."

Stasia was right. Neither of them was dating any-one steadily, and neither of them had ever had much of a complaint about it. But just lately Aimee had started to think maybe she wanted something more.

Like Mark Hyde? Sure, he looked good in that massive football player kind of way, and she knew he had depths she had just started to see. But it was complicated. Sometimes he was like a wounded animal she wanted to make better: sometimes she just wanted to put him out of his misery. Now and then she looked at him and got all thrilled by his proximity.

What? I have a danger addiction now?

And maybe that was the problem. Maybe she did.

Shane gave Kimmie a momentary smile, but the wounded expression on her face made him cringe and turn away. If anyone had ever told him he would've dated a girl as gorgeous as Kimmie—a cheerleader, as absurd as that was—and then broken up with her and that she'd *care* . . . He just couldn't believe she was still upset. It was weird, but it was also uncomfortable. Especially tonight, with Stasia just ten feet away from him.

"So where's this party tonight?" Shane said, interrupting his own thoughts.

Jekyll cleared his throat and looked his way. "Alicia D'Agostino's. Her folks are out of town."

That caught Shane's attention. "Whoa. That soon after Chad?"

Chad Johnson had been Alicia's boyfriend. Only a few weeks earlier he'd driven his car into the Hudson River during a party in the park. Most people figured it was a sudden suicidal fit, but Shane and his friends were pretty sure the incident had been connected to the creepy gremlins who'd created all kinds of trouble until they figured out how to stop them.

Jekyll shrugged. "Her sister, Andi, thought it was time for her to vent some steam."

The D'Agostino sisters were Italian beauties. Both had wild dark hair and were curvy in all the right ways. They were also from a family that really didn't much like the idea of parties. Shane knew it said a lot if they were going to risk their father's wrath for a good time.

"Works for me." He smiled at Jekyll. "Any party in a storm."

"See? I knew you'd lighten up eventually."

Shane was about to say more when they heard noises from down the street. They were almost at the top of Main Street, and they had a phenomenal view of the rest of the festivities spread all along the road down the hill.

"Something's going on down there," Hyde said, pointing.

But Shane had already noticed the commotion near the bottom of the hill. A cart loaded with

Halloween jewelry and a scattering of glow sticks and plastic odds and ends had gone over on its side, spilling orange and black junk jewelry all over the asphalt.

"What the hell?" Jekyll said. He was watching the action too. "A little overboard with the Halloween mischief, huh?"

And then the laughter crawled up the street, a cackling, cawing noise like crows screaming over a fresh meal. They'd all heard it before, in a cornfield where a kid named Adam Weiss had managed to choke to death on several ears of corn that had been rammed down his throat and where Missy Sterns barely escaped after being scratched and wounded.

The creatures that had made those sounds had been unsettling, demonic-looking things that had grown from the corn in the fields. They were vicious monsters that seemed determined to cause harm and chaos, but Shane and Aimee and Stasia had gone back to try to destroy them and instead had found an empty field. Shane thought the harvest of the corn had gotten rid of them.

He'd been wrong. Shane frowned as he moved downhill, not giving any thought to his safety. If the harvest spirits were back, he wanted to confirm it for himself.

Down the street, where the noise was coming from, several people let out cries of outrage, fear, or pain. He picked up his pace, though he couldn't see much through the crowds yet and a lot of people were blocking the way, also trying to see what was going on. Then Hyde lost his patience and carved through the crowd like an icebreaker through frozen seas. He pushed and the mass of people parted. Sometimes it was nice having a bulldozer for a friend.

Jekyll was behind them, and he knew Stasia and Aimee would be following as well, but he couldn't wait for them.

The screams were getting louder, and not just because Shane and his friends were closer. Whatever was making the noise down the hill was raging and ready for action. The road was blocked off for the festival at both ends and along the side streets. That was a good thing, because people were running blindly from whatever was down there. It would have been a disaster if a car came along.

The closer they got, the thicker the chaos became. A little kid in a Spider-Man mask let out a shriek and vanished a second later, yanked back into the crowd he was trying to get away from, and Shane pushed himself to move faster.

He took seven more paces toward the vanished grade-schooler before his feet got yanked out from under him. Shane caught himself on his palms even as he was reeled backward like a rabbit caught in a snare, pulled under a big cart where vendors had been selling cotton candy. He couldn't get any glimpse of what had grabbed him, but he had a pretty good idea.

"Shane!" Jekyll shouted, grabbing at his hands, yanking him back into the street. A child ran over Shane's back in an effort to escape the laughing things down the way. Then Shane looked over his shoulder and saw the thing that had dragged him.

It was a jack-o'-lantern, its face warped and distorted and moving as it screamed with laughter. A thick greenish tongue licked from the cavernous mouth as it scrabbled backward, at the same time drawing him closer once again. The hands and body under that pumpkin head seemed to be made of thick, hard vines, and the fingers that clutched at his ankles felt strong enough to snap his bones.

The crowd was so thick with people in costume, some genuinely running and others just moving up the hill in blind confusion, that no one seemed to notice the creature grasping Shane's legs. At night, in the chaos, most of them would have thought it was some guy in a costume anyway.

Shane twisted around and started kicking and pulling at green fingers, trying to break them loose.

"Get off me!" He managed to wrestle a finger away from his leg and bent it back until it snapped, splintering like a fresh green twig. The pumpkin face hissed and lunged forward, the slits of its eyes looming closer.

That was when Jekyll punted and caved in half of the thing's head. He drew back his leg for another shot and the creature let go of Shane, roaring as it turned to face the new threat.

Shane pushed away from the thing and started to rise, only to have someone run into him. They both hit the ground, but the woman who had knocked him over was up and moving before he could even see her face.

The crowd was breaking like a wave set to overrun the shoreline. Problem was, Shane and Jekyll were the shoreline. Just standing back up was proving to be a problem. Shane managed, but not without pushing a man back to give himself room. The man he'd shoved let out an indignant yelp and looked about ready to swing at him. Then his eyes went wide, and it was obvious he'd seen the pumpkin head attacking Steve. The guy took off, plunging back into the tide.

Shane was about to help Jekyll when he heard his sister scream.

He spun around, searching the crowd, and spotted Stasia and Aimee a little way up the road, trying to fend off a seriously deformed pumpkin head that was grabbing at them. His sister and his girlfriend both slapped its hands away, but it kept swinging its long, vicious-looking fingers, trying to grab them. This one had a face almost like a storybook witch's—with a long, hooked nose and a tapering chin, a shape that a normal pumpkin never would have taken—and even though it was grown from a different crop, he could recognize that he had seen it before in the cornfield. The similarity wasn't just his imagination. These were the same creatures they'd dealt with before. They'd been in the corn harvest last time and now had somehow grown themselves new bodies from the pumpkin crop.

But, looking around to make sure he knew where everyone was, Shane realized that there were more of the harvest spirits now—a *lot* more of them.

He would have gone to help Aimee and Stasia, but they had the thing down on the pavement and Stasia was kicking its pumpkin head with her heel. The pumpkin shattered.

One of the things jumped out of the crowd and landed on a kid who couldn't have been more than ten years old, judging by size. It was hard to tell under the Darth Vader outfit the boy was wearing. He let out a piercing scream and fell flat to the ground with the thing pinning him as soon as he landed. It pulled at the Vader mask and the kid started screaming louder, kicking and trying to reach around to hit the monster on its back but not landing any effective blows.

Aimee got there before Shane could and returned the favor, kicking the mass of hard vines and knocking it on its side. The outraged cawing noise it made was echoed several times by the others around them, and finally the crowd thinned out enough for Shane to realize how badly outnumbered they were.

This wasn't going at all the way he wanted it to. The things were getting meaner. One of them grabbed Shane by his hair and pulled him forward, forcing him to stagger in order to keep his scalp firmly attached to his skull.

He went with the momentum and slammed into the wiry thing, pushing hard to knock it down. Somewhere up ahead he heard Hyde let out a roar and glanced up to see his friend falling down in a jumble of the things. There had to be at least five of them crawling over him like rats on a piece of driftwood.

The trickster that had hold of Shane let out a cackling laugh and tried to push its thumbs through his eyes. He managed to duck but left himself exposed in the process. He knew, just knew, that it was going to hit him hard enough to knock the wind out of his sails for a few minutes.

And as he watched the rising tide of the things coming into the street and knocking aside people and Halloween decorations alike, he knew a few minutes was probably longer than he had to live.

Hyde went down hard, the things crawling on him and beating at his body savagely. Aimee ran toward him with Stasia at her side.

Aimee grabbed at the seemingly solid back of one of the creatures and cringed as the vines that it was built of moved in separate directions. It wasn't nearly as dense as she expected, and the leaves and runners on the vines tried to clutch at her flesh. The head of the thing turned almost all the way around, and it let out a loud caw that made her shiver.

Stasia grabbed at its talon as it kept turning, before it could grab Aimee. "Get off him, you freak!"

The thing turned on Stasia, shoving her back, but Hyde's boot against the side of its head stopped it short. The gourd caved in with a bass drumbeat, and though the blow would surely have crippled or killed a human being, the trickster spirit remained unfazed by the damage.

Hyde cursed loudly, then struck out, and one of the things went sailing. It was a good shot, but they were all over him.

Aimee wanted to help, but then the one with the missing face jumped on Stasia and let out another bloodcurdling screech. Stasia matched it scream for scream as it hooked a handful of her hair and started pulling.

Not too far away, she heard Shane and Jekyll both shouting, but Aimee could do nothing to help them. Her heartbeat thundered in her ears.

No. It wasn't her heart. The sound was coming from off to the left, and it wasn't her pulse.

It was hard, fast hoofbeats.

Aimee turned and felt her world go gray for a second.

They had made a lot of progress toward the bottom of the hill as they moved toward the disturbance, so she had a great view of the Headless Horseman as he charged down Main Street, the hooves of his stallion striking sparks on the road.

Acephelos leaned over his mount, riding hard, his left hand on the reins and his right hand whipping his saber in a tight arc. If people had been panicked by the attack of the pumpkin heads, they went into a screaming stampede when they saw the Horseman Killer bearing down on them at high speed. Those who had remained calm before gave up any pretense of being rational and ran and dove for cover. The path cleared in front of the charger as the Horseman slashed out with his weapon and cleaved one of the trickster spirits completely in half. The lower part of the thing stayed on the ground, but the upper portion was carried by the impact and slammed into a popcorn stand, spilling hot grease and popping kernels all over the road and on two people who'd been frozen in place by the unexpected spectacle.

Aimee kept staring, petrified. The last time she'd seen the Horseman had been when he was trying to kill her.

The Horseman and his steed turned toward her, moving even faster. Just like that, she remembered what her legs were for and bolted, grabbing Stasia's wrist and pulling for all she was worth.

Acephelos's saber flashed again, and the arm of the thing that was trying pull Stasia's scalp off fell away from the rest of its body. The massive bulk of the black horse hit the shrieking thing and slammed it to the ground hard enough to splatter rotten pumpkin across the pavement.

Then the Horseman was past, moving through the screaming crowd and charging for the main gathering of pumpkin monsters. Hyde had just managed to stand, two of the things still clinging to him like ticks on a dog—when the Horseman rode by. The horse brushed him roughly and sent him sprawling, bulldozing him off his feet.

Hyde let out a grunt and rolled as he hit the ground, spilling the things on his back in the process. Neither of the creatures had a chance to recover before the Horseman was on them, the blade in his hand carving through them like a thresher. They screamed as they died, hacked to death with terrifying speed.

Close by, Shane let out a panicked cry of recognition, and Aimee looked his way as the Horseman charged again. Shane did the smart thing: he crouched low and ran.

Then she realized he wasn't just fleeing the Horseman. Shane reached for a little girl who was trying to get away from one of the tricksters as it loomed over her and gnashed its carved pumpkin teeth. Even as he reached for the girl, the monster returned the favor, swiping at his face with sharp wooden fingers. Shane narrowly missed having the tip of his nose removed as he ducked.

The trickster wasn't quite as fast, and its head was severed a second later as the Horseman shot past. The gourd bounced and rolled, wobbling past Shane and all the way over to where Jekyll was standing.

Steve didn't even notice. His eyes were focused solely on the Horseman as the rider pulled the reins of his stallion and the horse reared, neighing loudly, while the Horseman seemed to look around, his body craning as if he had a head to turn on his shoulders.

Jekyll's eyes grew wider as he saw the Headless Horseman for the first time. Both Shane and Stasia had tried to explain how terrifying the Horseman was, but they probably hadn't done him justice. It wasn't merely that he had no head. There was so much more to it than that. Even standing perfectly still, Acephelos dripped menace. There was an air of deadly intent about the demon that none of the other things they had encountered so far came anywhere near matching. It wasn't just that he could take your head: it was something that made it clear killing you would only be the beginning of the things he would do.

The Legend of Sleepy Hollow inspired fear with his mere presence.

Then Jekyll, who had proved himself brave a dozen times in Aimee's eyes, forgot everything in the world except fear. His eyes were wide and his mouth agape as the Horseman turned again and charged directly at him.

But Acephelos wasn't after Jekyll. He turned the horse and started back down the hill the way he'd come, his arm in constant motion as he hacked his way through the few trickster spirits that hadn't fled in time. The creatures let out thunderous screams as they realized they were in the path of the charging demon. Then they scattered, moving faster than anything human.

Without the creatures attacking them, Shane and Jekyll worked their way to Aimee's side. Stasia was a few feet away, staring at the Horseman, the severed arm of the hair-pulling trickster in her hands. Thick dark fluids drooled from the stump; she'd never seen anything like that come out of a pumpkin.

The Horseman paused and turned slightly in the saddle, the saber in his gloved hand pointing up toward the bloated moon and the scattered clouds.

Then he looked at them.

He had no head, he had no eyes, but he looked at them. And Aimee was sure that he recognized them.

Hyde moved in front of her and Stasia, as if he could possibly stop the Horseman from killing them. She noticed the blood on Mark's hands. His own, she was sure. This time.

The Horseman turned in his seat and jabbed his heels at the flanks of the black stallion underneath him. The horse bolted forward and veered left, following the largest group of fleeing tricksters.

All around them the noises of the carnival had broken into the cries of children and the shocked voices of teens and adults too stunned to fully understand what had happened around them.

"So, that was Acephelos?" Jekyll's voice was very shaky and two octaves higher than usual.

Shane nodded emphatically. "Yep. Oh, yeah. That's him."

Hyde dropped what remained of a pumpkin from his closed fists. "Figures. He's a wuss," he said, voice full of false bravado.

Stasia snorted and shot a lopsided grin in his direction. "How do you figure that was a wuss?"

Hyde didn't smile. His expression didn't change at all as he watched the figure of the Horseman climb into the thickest part of the woods.

"He cheated. He used a sword."

There it was: the faintest hint of a grin curled the left side of his lip. Before Aimee could come up with a response, they heard the warbling cry of police sirens coming their way.

"Let's go. We're out of here." Hyde didn't give them a chance to decide for themselves but started ushering them in the direction they'd come from. "Don't want anything to do with the cops."

CHAPTER TWO

THE D'AGOSTINOS LIVED in a nice house with what Shane was certain was the world's largest backyard. Jekyll's family had a mansion that was easily three times the size of Alicia and Andi's house, but his yard was a postage stamp in comparison. High school kids were milling all over the lawn, taking advantage of all the space.

A boom box in the corner was blasting out something with a hyperactive beat and the most repetitive lyrics Shane had ever heard. Bubblegum pop usually made him want to puke, but tonight somehow the beat was what he needed. Maybe Stasia was rubbing off on him; not that he was complaining.

They'd briefly debated going home. All of them were tempted to call it a night. But they were all too pumped with adrenaline to sleep, and it seemed like a good idea to stick together, at least for a while, after what had happened on Main Street. Not that there was anything they could really do about it.

27

What had gone down tonight was in the cops' hands now.

And the Horseman's.

As they made their way over to the party, they'd talked about how freaky it was that Horseman was back and that instead of killing anyone—especially instead of killing any of *them*—he'd helped. Tonight, at least, the Horseman was on their side.

"Looks like half the school is here," Shane said, glancing around the backyard. He was a little surprised. He hadn't really done that many parties since hitting Sleepy Hollow—or before that, either.

Stasia looked his way with a tolerant smile. Aimee shook her head, and Jekyll answered, "Amateur. This is nothing."

"Then *something* must be one hell of a sight."

Hyde looked his way and shrugged. "It'll do."

Shane watched Mark look over the crowd and then stand up straighter. His friend's face went into its normal stony expression and his eyes narrowed just a little, like he was waiting for something to go wrong. In Hyde's defense, something went wrong a lot.

They hadn't actually joined the masses that were moving through the backyard and breaking into smaller clumps of people. They planned to, but Shane wanted to wait until they were all a little calmer. Not that he really expected it to happen, but he could dream.

"Okay, so why is the Horseman back?" Aimee asked, looking at him like he was supposed to have the answers. He didn't.

"Maybe because of the pact," Stasia suggested, keeping her voice low and her back to the rest of the party. "He got what he wanted from us when we met in the cemetery, so maybe he decided to honor the pact he made with the town founders."

"Not sure how much sense that makes. He didn't help us out with the naiads or the gremlins. I hope you're right, though," Shane said. "I don't much like the alternative."

"What's the alternative?" Hyde asked, his eyes already looking over the crowd in the backyard.

"That he's saving us for later."

Jekyll and Hyde hadn't been there the first time the Horseman had come after them, but they knew the score. Ichabod Crane had summoned Acephelos to keep the other demons and creatures he had brought into Sleepy Hollow in check. The spell called for Crane to sacrifice himself, inviting the ancient, headless demon, Acephelos, to use his body as a host. But Crane had reneged and killed the mayor of Sleepy Hollow, using the dead man to take his place in the ritual.

Problem was, that meant Acephelos—the Headless Horseman—didn't have to hold up his side of the bargain.

Crane left town. The demon rampaged through the Hollow, forcing the town founders to strike a bargain. None of Crane's bloodline was ever to be allowed to settle in the town again. In return the Horseman would do what he was summoned to do—keep evil and the supernatural out of Sleepy Hollow. If the founders or their descendents ever broke the agreement, he'd bring his wrath down on them and shatter whatever mystical gates kept the evil away.

It had worked, too, until Aimee and Shane had come to the town and inadvertently brokeup the pact. They were Crane's descendants, but no one knew that, and even if they had, the curse had been forgotten a hundred years ago.

Everything the Headless Horseman had kept locked away had been freed when they came to town. That was the main reason they kept their eyes open and tried to know what was coming to cause trouble next. Shane and Aimee figured that it was sort of their fault all of this horrible stuff was happening in the Hollow, and their ancestor was the one who'd started it all. Somebody had to try to stop it, to keep the town safe.

Family obligations sucked.

That he's saving us for later, Shane had said. Hyde rolled his eyes. "That's what I like about you, Shane," he said. "Your optimism."

"Hey, enough of that for tonight." Jekyll thumped

them both on their shoulders. "There's a party going on, and I intend to take full advantage of it."

"Is there anything you wouldn't take full advantage of, Steve?" Aimee started down the grassy slope and into the thick of the party, with Stasia right beside her.

Jekyll pretended to think about it for a second. "Not that I've come across."

Shane laughed and decided to worry about the Horseman later. It had been almost two weeks since they'd all had time to get together and just hang out. For once, Shane had decided to relax. If he'd given it a moment's thought, he would have realized that couldn't last.

Aimee was doing her best to keep it light. She wanted a beer, and she wanted to dance and party and forget all about the Horseman and the pumpkin heads that had caused so much trouble at the festival. Best to stick to that plan as long as she could because she knew all of that chaos was just the beginning of something, not the end. The Horseman hadn't just shown up for no reason. Something was brewing, and it wasn't going to be anything good.

Shane sidled up next to her, hands jammed in his pockets. He was supposed to be enjoying the party, but she could see the trouble in his eyes. "So, you figure we're screwed when Dad hears about the Horseman?"

"I'm not moving out of this town, Shane. Just remember that when the fighting starts."

"You think it's going to get that bad that fast?"

"Yeah. I do. I think moving is the first suggestion he's going to make."

"Well, I'm with you on this. We're not moving." He looked away, and she saw his jaw tense up. "I don't feel like starting over anywhere else. This is home now. I mean, I had friends back in Boston, but not like here. I want to stay. And besides, we have obligations."

"Preaching to the choir, big brother. Wasn't our fault, but we brought all this on. No way can I leave Stasia and Ella and Turner and the guys to face all this without me. Not when we're the reason."

"I know." He shrugged. "And who knows what would happen if we left? It could even get worse."

Aimee shook her head and smiled. "Not sure if that's possible." She grabbed a beer from a large cooler. It was cold in her hand, and it felt nice and familiar, but she didn't open it. She wasn't really in the mood to get drunk. She just wanted to relax.

Shane eyed the beer but kept his mouth shut. That was good. They were slowly starting to accept the boundaries of their relationship since Mom had died. It had recently been pointed out to her that she could be a little too controlling of her brother's life. Not that she meant to be, but her mother's death had instilled in her a need to protect her family.

She looked over at Hyde and saw him glowering at a jock from the school. The jock, Mike Demeter, was doing his very best not to wither and die under the glare.

There wasn't any reason for Hyde to shoot looks at Mike. It was just, like, a hobby or something. Scaring jocks was how he had a good time.

Shane was right. Half the school seemed to be here, and most of the kids had been drinking like fish. Several members of the football team were making asses of themselves, but they were all laughing. In a fit of solidarity they'd all dressed as themselves. Almost everyone else had made at least a token effort to wear a costume.

Derek Van Brunt was among the jocks, and he was already slurring, listing like a drunken sailor when he walked. Derek was very, very drunk and currently looking for someone to dance with. It was obvious his girlfriend, Erin Ingalsby, wanted no part of that.

Only a fool could have missed the frost between Erin and Derek tonight. Erin was leaning against a picnic table in the backyard, her arms crossed over her chest. Her bottom lip was in a pout, and her eyes were narrowed down to slits as she glared at the small gathering of jocks that surrounded Derek.

Aimee turned away and saw Shane and Stasia standing together a short distance away. She went to join them. Jekyll was already mingling, and Hyde was back the way she'd come, still looking menacingly at the jock he'd targeted.

Another song started up, and Aimee let herself sway lightly to the music. Jekyll rejoined them, looking a bit disgruntled.

"What's up?" Aimee asked him.

"This party." He scowled and looked around. "You ever go to a party and just know it wasn't going to end well?"

"You mean like cops, unexpected parents, and all of that?"

"Yeah, like that," Jekyll agreed.

Aimee nodded.

"Well, either I'm more freaked out than I thought I was by your buddy down at the carnival or my spider sense is telling me this is going to be one of those parties."

Aimee cast a look at Shane and Stasia, but they were talking quietly to each other and hadn't noticed Jekyll's approach. Hyde had seemed to notice that something was troubling his buddy and left off menacing Mike Demeter to drift back toward the group.

"You think we should leave?" She almost sounded

hopeful, even to her own ears. Somehow the idea of getting ripped and dancing all night had lost its appeal for the evening. Maybe they'd all been kidding themselves, thinking they could just go on and enjoy themselves like it was any ordinary evening.

"I think it might be for the best, yeah. I mean, maybe hang for a few minutes but after that, head out."

She looked at Hyde, who shrugged his beefy shoulders. He was good either way.

Aimee walked over and tapped Stasia. She didn't know what Shane had been talking to her about, but whatever it was, they seemed ultra-serious.

"Hey, guys. Jekyll's getting a bad vibe, and the jocks are already acting like monkeys. Wanna blow this place?"

Stasia looked from her to Hyde and Jekyll and then to the gathered kids. Then she glanced at Shane. "We could get a pizza and watch a movie or something."

Shane nodded. He was pretty agreeable to anything that didn't involve partying on most nights anyway.

"Cool," Aimee said, turning to Jekyll. "Let's go."

They started to walk back up the hill toward the D'Agostinos' front yard. While they'd been talking, though, Derek had weaved a drunken path toward them. He'd heard the last of their conversation and saw them ready to leave, and he reached out and grabbed Aimee's arm, still apparently in search of a dance partner.

"Come on, you guys just got here. It's a party! Come dance with me."

Derek's smile looked like it was ready to slide off his face, and his breath smelled like a brewery accident. Normally Aimee thought he was cute in spite of being an asshole. Tonight the cute part was nowhere to be found.

"No, thanks. We're gonna head out." She added a dash of venom to her glare and then looked pointedly at Erin. "Besides, you have a date, remember?"

He completely ignored her second comment and turned instead to look at Stasia. "Come on, Stasia. Dance with me."

Stasia flashed a smile and shook her head. "Maybe some other time."

"What? Has hanging around with Shane rubbed off on you? Or doesn't your boyfriend let you dance with real men?"

Stasia stepped back. "Excuse me?" The tone of her voice dropped the temperature by a good ten degrees.

Erin stepped forward while Aimee was trying to absorb what he'd just said. It wasn't the words so much as the way they were spoken. Derek said it with conviction, like he had every reason in the world to believe that her best friend and her brother were dating. He said it casually, not as a jab at Shane.

"Come on, Stasia! You're the party girl around here; come on and party with me." Derek's smile was looking a little more off than before, and he was almost sneering now, his voice more aggressive.

Erin put a hand on his shoulder. "Derek, you're being an asshole—stop it."

Derek shrugged her hand away from his arm. "What? I'm wrong? You went from the hottest thing in town to the bride of the loser, Stasia. Come on, show me you still have what it takes to make guys happy."

It was inevitable. Hyde stepped in.

He reached for Derek, grabbed a fistful of the drunken jock's hair, and hauled him up so he was standing straight for the first time that night. Derek let out a grunt of pain and anger and leered at Hyde.

"Go on, dude. I can't feel a goddamn thing."

Hyde glanced back at Stasia, who shook her head. Aimee was surprised. She was sorely tempted to tell Hyde to beat the crap out of Derek, no matter what Stasia wanted. But Hyde would have done it, and he hated that part of himself.

With a sneer, Hyde let go. Derek staggered toward Stasia, who just drew back in revulsion.

"Wow. Beer makes you such a charmer."

Derek laughed. "What, you're going from town slut to little miss ice queen?" The alcohol had apparently removed what few brain cells he had. "I'm just asking for a dance, not for a—"

"Derek! Stop it!" Erin was angry now, and Aimee understood why. Aimee had always known there was something in the past between Stasia and Derek, but now he was getting belligerent.

"What?!" He shot a hard look at Erin, and she stepped back.

Stasia started to turn away from him, disgusted and angry and yes, Aimee saw it: there was a guilty expression on her face when her eyes met Aimee's.

All through the exchange Shane had stood silently, his face flushing and his jaw set with fury. His fists were balled up beside him. He was usually the one to try the calm route, to be the peacemaker. Tonight he looked like he was going to explode.

"You're done, Derek," Shane said, and it wasn't a question. "Let it go."

Aimee stared at him. *Damn, can I be that stupid? Shane and Stasia? What the hell?*

"You don't walk away from me, Stasia!" Derek pushed past Shane, deliberately hitting him with his shoulder in the process. "Come on, Stasia. Why don't you tell your new boyfriend all about what we used to be like together? Let him know the real you before you go all exclusive."

Shane shook his head, his expression darker than Aimee had ever seen. Normally Derek would have torn him apart. But drunk as the jock was, Shane might do him some damage if he set out to.

Stasia glared. "You shut your mouth, Derek."

"Well, you never shut yours." He was grinning now, an ugly, mean smile. She'd seen the same look on Hyde's face, only with Derek it was almost worse because it was unexpected.

Hyde uncrossed his arms and moved in that direction, following the action with his eyes. "You don't want to say anything else, Derek. I mean it."

"Kiss my ass, Hyde."

Hyde bristled at the comment and took another step toward the jock.

Aimee finally spoke. She was confused by what was going on, if there was anything going on, between Shane and Stasia, but Stasia was still her best friend.

"Don't even listen to him, guys. He's just making a fool of himself." She kept her voice cold and level.

Derek's head turned fast, and his hand followed. He'd barely even gotten, "Shut it, bitch!" out of his mouth before his palm slapped Aimee across the mouth.

Aimee's head snapped back and her face went numb for half a second before the pain started.

By the time she could have reacted, it was too

late. Hyde would have broken the sorry bastard, but Shane beat him to it. Her brother slammed his fist into Derek's face with the only real punch she'd ever seen him throw, solid and without hesitation. Derek stepped back, his lip already split and bleeding, and shook his head.

"Nobody does that, you bastard!" Shane roared, shaking with rage. "Nobody touches my sister."

Shane wasn't done. He was heading for Derek again, and drunk as he was, Derek got ready to fight back. Aimee started toward them, ready to beat Derek down herself, but Hyde reached out and stopped her. She looked up, ready to protest, and remembered what he'd said before about how she'd humiliated Shane on the first day of school. And she got it. Aimee had embarrassed Shane by sticking up for him. Tonight it was him sticking up for her, taking back some of what he hadn't been able to live down since that day.

Shane took another swing, and Derek side-stepped before slamming a fist into her brother's rib cage. Shane grunted and swung again, this time landing a good shot to Derek's stomach. Then Derek ran at him, his face purple with fury. The blow lifted Shane off the ground and then they were both on the lawn, rolling over and swinging at each other, screaming and cursing and grunting as they fought.

Several of the jocks looked ready to interfere.

Hyde cleared his throat loudly and shook his head at them. They stayed where they were.

Derek landed a solid punch along Shane's cheek, and he closed his eye as the jock's knuckles went across the edge of it. Then Shane started swinging hard and fast, and the fight was all his. After a few blows in the face Derek stopped fighting and started trying to defend himself.

Hyde stood next to her, watching, not saying a word. Stasia looked his way.

"Make him stop, Mark."

Aimee nodded. "Yeah. Please, end it."

Hyde walked over, grabbing Shane under his armpits and physically lifting him off Derek. Derek blinked and looked at Shane with pure hatred in his eyes but apparently lacked the energy to do anything about it. His face was already swelling in a few places.

Shane, still off the ground and struggling against Hyde's intervention, spat a stream of blood from his mouth. "You *ever* touch her again and I swear to God, they'll have to peel you off the ground!"

Hyde set him down and immediately blocked his attempt to get back over to Derek. "That's enough. It's done."

When Shane tried moving around him a second time, Hyde grabbed his shoulders and forced his friend to look him in the eyes. "It's over, Shane. Calm down."

Jekyll put a hand on Aimee's arm and one on Stasia's and led them away from the party while Hyde took care of marching Shane along. Behind them the music had stopped and a large crowd was watching Derek as he rolled over and got to his hands and knees, coughing and trying to catch his breath.

Jekyll shook his head as they walked away, trying to put a little lighter spin on things. "See? This is why I never take Shane anywhere. He's always looking to kick someone's ass."

He shut up when no one laughed.

Shane looked a bit dazed and a lot pissed off. Stasia was staring at the ground, her expression deeply troubled. Aimee had never seen her friend brood before.

She had to figure out what the hell was going on between her brother and her best friend. Because much as she hated to think it, something was definitely going on.

Could Shane and Stasia be an item? Half an hour ago she'd have laughed at the idea, but the more she thought about it, the more she realized it wouldn't be that hard for them to pull off without her knowing. Stasia and Aimee both worked at the same place, but they didn't work together every night. Weekdays it was normally one or the other of them working. Weekends it was both of them, but not always on the same shift. So even though she spent a lot of time with Stasia, there were plenty of times when they barely saw each other outside of school.

Her brother was her brother and she loved him, but they had argued their whole lives, and that had always created a distance between them. They still fought, but what they'd faced together in Sleepy Hollow had brought them together. They were finally beginning to actually like each other.

And now this. Shane knew how she felt about him dating her friends. And Stasia . . . How had they kept this from her?

Aimee was trying not to get angry. She really was.

Hyde put one of his massive hands on her shoulder. "You all right, Aimee?"

He looked down at her, his expression genuinely concerned.

"Yeah. I guess so." She shot a look at her brother's back.

"Don't be so rough on him, okay? Let them talk to you about it before you get angry."

She nodded, and Hyde cracked a rare smile. "Listen, me and Steve are gonna bug out. You sure you're okay?"

"You're leaving?"

He shrugged. "Yeah, we figure you could use a little time to talk without us around."

She did her best to smile, and a moment later he and Jekyll were heading in a different direction.

She looked at Shane and Stasia, taking the time to really study their faces. "So, you two are an item?"

Had Shane ever looked so guilty in their entire lives? She didn't think so. Stasia's expression was harder to read, but neither of them turned away.

Stasia spoke first. "Sort of. But it's not like Derek said, okay?"

Aimee shrugged, her eyes never leaving Stasia's until her friend started to look very uncomfortable.

Shane sighed and took a step toward her. "Aimee. Listen, it wasn't exactly something we planned. . . ."

Aimee tried not to make a scene. She looked at her brother and then back at Stasia and bit her lower lip to stop from saying something she'd regret later. Instead she just nodded and moved across the street toward the front of their house. If she ran the last few steps, it wasn't because she meant to but only because she needed to think, and she didn't trust herself not to turn into a drama queen right then and there.

She felt their eyes on her back as she opened the front door and slid inside, looking back only briefly at the two of them. They wanted to talk, she could see it, but she wasn't ready. They could talk later, when she didn't feel betrayed. And not just that, but stupid. How could she not have seen it?

Aimee went up to her room and closed the door. No one knocked, and no one entered.

Really, that was what she'd been expecting. Her brother and her best friend had other things to worry about.

CHAPTER THREE

IT DIDN'T SEEM like it could be almost time for his curfew, but the watch on his wrist wasn't lying, and Shane knew he'd be in deep trouble if his father beat him home.

It didn't take a genius to know something big was going down in Sleepy Hollow, and his father would want him home on time, especially since the cops were likely to assume that the Horseman Killer was roaming the streets again. They were right, of course. They just didn't know how right.

Even so, it took a lot of willpower to make himself do the right thing and just walk Stasia home. After the night they'd had, he wanted more than ever to just hold on to her. No matter how much time they got to spend alone with each other, Shane always wanted more, afraid that at any moment something could happen that would change things between them.

"So, I'll see you tomorrow?" Stasia sounded doubtful. They'd both talked about telling Aimee a dozen times, worried about hurting her feelings and hating that they were doing things behind her back, but now that they'd been outed by that dumbass Van Brunt, Stasia was afraid the rules had changed.

They hadn't. Shane's sister would just have to deal. It was too early to know if he was really, really in love—how could he know if he'd never felt it before?—but Shane figured he'd never know if he let Aimee dictate who he could see. And he wanted to know almost desperately. He wanted to know without doubt that it wasn't just infatuation.

"Unless my dad skins me for being late or Aimee takes an ax to me." He tried to make it a joke, but it didn't quite work. Stasia smiled anyway.

One last kiss, long and lingering and bittersweet for it being the last of the night, and then he was on his way. He left Stasia's house and started down the road, one ear pricked and waiting for the sound of hoofbeats clomping down the street behind him.

Instead he heard the distinct sound of his father's station wagon as it moved in his direction.

He almost would have preferred Acephelos.

The car pulled up next to him, and his father's window rolled down. "Get in the car." Oh, yes, Alan Lancaster was not pleased.

Shane didn't even think about arguing but got in on the passenger side quickly and quietly.

"You want to tell me what the hell you're doing

walking out here after what happened earlier? And don't even pretend you don't know."

"I had to walk Stasia home, Dad."

"It doesn't take two hours to walk home!"

"Dad, it wasn't that big a deal."

"It was big enough, Shane. Don't try to downplay it. I know about how you got the bruise on your jaw and I know you were at the Harvest Festival, okay? Mrs. Hoskins from the Bookmark saw you and Aimee and your crew."

"Dad, I just needed—"

"Shane, damn it, the Horseman Killer went down Main Street and started chopping away! Don't think for even an instant I'm forgetting that he was after you and your sister and Stasia too. I think you going on a date is secondary to that. Are we understanding each other here?"

Despite the anger in his voice—which mostly hid the worry—Alan drove calmly. That, combined with the way he was acting, the way he was glossing over the goblins that had been running rampant at the festival, told Shane what he and Aimee had already been suspecting. His dad might not know everything that was going on, but he was beginning to suspect.

It was what his father wasn't saying that was the giveaway. He wasn't talking about the weirdness of the pumpkin things—that had to have been seen by dozens of people. Most would say it was punks or gangbangers in costume, causing trouble. That was certainly what Chief Burroughs would say. But if Alan believed that, he would have at least mentioned them, and he hadn't. He also wasn't talking about the fact that the Horseman hadn't killed a single person. But Shane knew his father was aware of those facts. His father was the editor of the *Sleepy Hollow Gazette*, and before that he'd worked as an investigative reporter in Boston. The man didn't miss details like those, and the only time he didn't speak of them to Shane and Aimee was when he was trying to hide something he found particularly unpleasant.

Shane didn't say much on the trip home. To balance out his silence, his father stayed quiet too.

When they pulled into the driveway of the house, Alan finally spoke again. "Get some sleep, Shane. We're not done discussing this, but it'll wait until tomorrow."

Shane nodded and kept his mouth shut. Aimee was already in bed when they went inside. Shane followed her example and went to his room. It was a long time before he finally managed to sleep. He kept thinking about everything that had happened, and his emotions ran from excited by it all to miserable with worry. In the end, he settled for sore. He might have won the fight with Derek, but his ribs were aching and his jaw was swollen and bruised.

• • •

Aimee scrambled the eggs and Shane made the toast. They set a place for their father and covered his breakfast with a second plate before they got around to reading the newspaper.

The article on the return of the Horseman Killer made the front page and really didn't leave any room for other stories. Shane and Aimee had agreed with as few words as possible that the issues between them could wait. Dealing with their father was first priority. They sat next to each other at the kitchen table and read the article carefully.

Aimee said it first, but it was on both of their minds. "He knows something. He has to. Even if he doesn't know, he knows something."

"Yeah." Shane finished reading the last part of the article, and he nodded as he spoke. "This is really, really close to what I remember. This is almost exactly what happened. That's . . . worrisome."

She was about to agree with her brother when her father came into the kitchen, already dressed for work.

"Okay, guys. Let's have a talk."

The siblings exchanged looks, both dreading what they knew was coming.

Aimee nodded. "You want to talk about last night?"

"Last night, and what's been going on in Sleepy Hollow almost since the minute we got into town." He walked to the far counter, his entire body rigid with tension. "A lot of strange things have happened in this town, and you and your friends have been around for more of them than I feel could be coincidence."

"Dad, we didn't exactly ask the Headless Horseman to come chasing after us," Shane said with a defensive look on his bruised face.

Alan poured himself a cup of coffee and ignored the breakfast they'd made for him. "Let's get down to it. You guys know more than you're letting on, and I want answers."

Aimee coughed into her hand. What he wanted was a big order, and more importantly, something that could make him go a little too parental for comfort. She and Shane had established themselves in town, and neither of them wanted to go anywhere else. Moving once was bad enough.

When neither of them spoke, he shook his head and set down the coffee. "Look, guys, I may be a pragmatist and a skeptic, but I'm not a fool. There've been things I could explain—a guy in a costume killing people is a lot easier to believe than a guy with no head—but there've been things I couldn't explain too. Things Burroughs is just too stubborn to even allow were odd. If there was no rational explanation for it—like what happened to those cattle out near the Delisle place and that boy who died in the cornfield at Ingalsby farm that night—well, it was easier to think there was something I and the police had missed than to allow for the possibility that maybe there were things we just weren't willing to believe in.

"Then, well . . ." their father said, his face turning pale. "After what happened at the grand opening of the theater, I knew it was more than just a few strange stories and a maniac in a headless horseman costume."

He looked right at Aimee and locked eyes with her. "I saw those things, whatever they were. It wasn't rats at the Capitol that night. You know it and I know it, and now it's time for us to compare notes. So come clean, guys."

Aimee looked at her brother and saw the same resignation she felt reflected in his face.

"Okay, Dad. But you might want to sit down for this. . . ."

They started talking. They told him about the truth behind "The Legend of Sleepy Hollow," about Ichabod Crane and his dabbling in dark magic, and about his betrayal of the town and its mayor. They told him about the demon Acephelos and the legend of the Headless Horseman and the curse on Sleepy Hollow involving descendants of Ichabod Crane.

They told him that they were of the Crane bloodline.

Shane filled him in on the research that had led them to the crypt where the Horseman's head was buried and how they had given him back his head and he had let them live. They explained that even so, the curse meant all the creatures of darkness had an engraved invitation to set up shop in the Hollow now, thanks to them. Aimee told him about the Whispering Tree. The two of them filled in the details about the naiads and explained what he hadn't known regarding the gremlins that had overrun the abandoned assembly plant.

Their father listened, asking a question when something wasn't clear and otherwise merely soaking in the details that they provided.

He handled it better than Aimee had expected.

"We're moving," he said with a deep note of resignation in his voice. Sleepy Hollow was his home too these days. Not just a place he had planned on passing through.

"Dad, no!"

"I didn't say it was open to discussion, Aimee. We're leaving Sleepy Hollow."

"It won't make a difference, Dad." Shane leaned back in his seat, his face as calm as if he were sitting down for a debate about the merits of coffee as opposed to sleep.

"You don't think so?"

"No, I don't. The Horseman could have had us last night if he was still after us. He didn't come hunting for us. He came for those freaky harvest spirits. He's back to doing what he was summoned to do in the first place. I don't know why now and not with the naiads or the gremlins, but there's no denying it. And that means, scary as he is, he isn't exactly one of the bad guys right now. Or at least he isn't acting the part."

"What? We're supposed to kick back and enjoy the show, Shane? He still killed people. Or did you forget that?" Their father shook his head, and Aimee felt her stomach drop.

"How could we forget?" she argued. "The point is, we don't know how to destroy him, but it sure looks like we've not only stopped him, but that he's actively helping people in the Hollow now. Doesn't mean he's not a monster, but he's no longer a threat."

"For the moment," Alan said dubiously.

"Dad, we're responsible for this," Shane said. "Not, like, directly. Obviously we never meant for any of this to happen. But we triggered the whole thing because, through Mom's family, we're related to Ichabod Crane. If any of his relatives had shown up back when Sleepy Hollow still believed all of this stuff, they would've been turned over to the Horseman and that would've been that. But too much time had gone by. No one remembered. They just didn't know. So we showed up, settled down in the Hollow, and boom. The pact was broken. Up until then the Horseman had kept his side of the deal, making sure none of the nasties got in. But we showed up and the deal was off, he let them go, or they escaped or something.

"That's changed now. We made some kind of peace or truce with him, I guess, giving him back his . . . y'know, his head." Shane shrugged at how crazy it sounded. "The point is, he's obviously back on the job now."

Their father scowled. "How is having a monster fighting other monsters supposed to make me want to stay in this town and risk all of our lives, Shane? I'm not getting that."

Aimee answered before Shane could. "We can't just leave, Dad. Not just because we're kind of responsible for this, but because we don't want to move again."

"Okay, even if the whole curse thing's true." Their dad held up a fast hand to stop the objections he was probably expecting in reaction to the comment. "Even if all of what you said is true, you're not responsible for this. Let's get that straight."

"But we are—"

"No, Shane, you're not. If I made an enemy through something I wrote in the paper, you wouldn't be responsible for that. And if that enemy took their anger out on you, would that be deserved? You two coming to town might have been a catalyst, but you didn't light the fuse on this powder keg."

"We were what caused the Horseman to come back, Dad," Aimee reminded him.

"No, Ichabod Crane did that. You just got stuck with the side effects."

Shane shook his head, and Aimee looked from her brother to her father. Sometimes it unsettled her how alike they were, especially when they got into a debate. "The genie's already out of the bottle, Dad, and if we leave, it won't change that."

"It'll change the likelihood of you two getting hurt."

"Dad, we have knowledge that helps us identify the threats and maybe even stop people from getting hurt. You and me and Aimee all know that it isn't the sort of thing most people would believe if you printed it, so it's kind of silly to think that a public announcement would keep people out of danger."

Shane started ticking points off on his fingers. "No one is gonna believe that a bunch of water sprites drowned anyone, and if you think anyone in town will believe gremlins started messing up cars and killing people, then maybe you should be working for the *National Enquirer*. 'Cause that's the only place that would hire you if you started running stories like that in the local paper. The mayor would drive you out of town, and we all know Burroughs is on so tight a leash that he'd drive you to the town line himself if the mayor said so."

Alan stared hard at his son for several heartbeats,

and Aimee wondered if her brother had stepped over the line.

Then their dad smiled, a small chuckle escaping his mouth as he nodded. "Okay, you make a good argument. I'm not making any promises, but I'll think about it. If there's a single incident where the Horseman harms anyone else in town, though, we're gone immediately. And there are going to be a few changes around here if we do stay."

Their father looked at each of them as if expecting an instant explosion of protests and seemed shocked when none were forthcoming.

He raised a finger. "Effective immediately, you don't walk anywhere after dark. Either I give you a ride or someone else does or you call a damned cab. No exceptions. If you're working, that's fine. But you do not walk home, and you sure don't walk home alone."

Aimee managed not to explode, but there were going to be serious issues with that as far as she was concerned. Still, she said, "Okay . . ."

"Also, if you see so much as a suspicious shadow moving down the sidewalk, I want to know about it. No more hiding these things from me. Fine, so I can't always report the truth about what's happening, but I want to know."

"That might make it easier to deal with Chief Burroughs," Shane suggested. "I mean, knowing the real story might make it easier to know what to say to him."

Alan raised an eyebrow. "So you two already know I've been sugarcoating some of the news for the chief?"

They both nodded.

"True enough," he admitted. "Burroughs has been incredibly frustrated. The man's more of a skeptic than even I am—or was—but the town council and the mayor have been breathing down his neck. So when he doesn't have all the answers and it doesn't look like there's any rational answer, he covers as best he can. Plus the town could be crippled by more scary media attention, never mind the panic."

"You think he really doesn't have a clue what's going on?" Aimee asked, amazed.

Her dad shook his head. "Most of us, we're not going to believe in werewolves unless we get bit and start growing fur ourselves."

He paused and stared at them. "There aren't really werewolves, are there?"

Shane shrugged. "Don't know."

"Haven't met any yet," Aimee explained.

"This is all going to take some getting used to." Their father sighed in amazement. "Anyway, Burroughs is the kind of man who'd fight the truth if it meant changing his view of the world. But all he really wants is to protect the Hollow. In being careful about how I play things in the paper, I've been trying to help him keep the peace. We all saw what happened here when the Horseman showed up. But from now on, what I can do is make sure that I warn people whenever possible and try to help figure out what is really going on in town. So no more secrets."

Shane nodded again, not saying a word. Reluctantly Aimee agreed and nodded too. Maybe it would work out. Either way, it beat moving.

Their father ate a hurried breakfast and gave them each a kiss on the forehead. He didn't get mushy too often, but the night before had obviously scared him more than he wanted to admit.

After he was gone, Shane sighed and propped his head in his hands. "Well, that didn't go as badly as it could have."

"I'm not complaining," Aimee said.

He shook his head and rolled his shoulders to ease some of the tension that had built since their father entered the room. "So, are we okay, Aimee?"

"What? You mean about you and Stasia?"

"Yeah."

"I don't know." She looked in his eyes, and he didn't look away. "I need time to think about it, Shane. You both kept it from me, which sucks. Besides, the whole thing is just so . . . annoying and inconvenient."

Shane tilted his head. "I don't get how it's inconvenient."

The sad part was, he probably didn't. So she enlightened him. "First, if I have a problem with my brother being an asshole, it's traditionally my best friend I bitch to about it. Now she might get all 'oh, he didn't mean it and you just don't understand him' with me and it's gonna piss me off. Second, she's my best friend, but she's your girlfriend, and if she has to choose between us when something important comes up and she chooses either way, one of us is gonna get bitchy. And I don't just mean me."

He nodded. "Yeah, I've been thinking about that. . . . We've even talked about it, Aimee. We didn't want to go behind your back, but you kind of have a record for getting postal over your friends and me."

"Duh, you think?"

Shane shrugged.

"We're okay, Shane. . . . It's just gonna take time for me to be comfortable with this."

They were silent for a minute. Then Aimee snorted and shook her head.

"Well," she said, "at least now I know why you dumped Kimmie Hill."

Shane turned red. "Yeah, that's pretty much it."

"I was kinda thinking maybe you were just gay and didn't know it." Aimee grinned.

He threw a piece of toast at her and she ducked. But they were both smiling again. Aimee was happy that in spite of everything, she and Shane were starting to be friends.

She just hoped it would stay that way.

CHAPTER
FOUR

NOT EVERY DAY brought bloodshed and insanity to Sleepy Hollow or the lives of its citizens. Two weeks passed with few incidents to mark the lives of the Lancasters. Shane and Stasia continued to date, continued to play it cool in front of Aimee as much as possible, and continued to sneak in a few minutes of heavy snogging whenever possible.

Daily life in the Hollow went on, just as it always had. Derek Van Brunt was still a jerk, and likely that would never change. He did apologize to Aimee when he saw her again, deeply embarrassed about the fact that he had hauled off and slapped a girl in front of his teammates. Though no one ever spoke about it, there was also a very real chance that he'd been threatened with bodily injury if he didn't. Not only by Erin—who watched from the sidelines while he apologized and never once stopped glaring at him until he was finished—but just possibly by Hyde, whom Derek was avoiding with a nearly religious fervor.

Derek and Erin almost broke up over that night. They had a long drawn-out screaming match over him being an idiot, but after two weeks they were finally at peace in their relationship again and ready to get in a little quality time together. November in Sleepy Hollow could be bitterly cold, but the day they chose to sneak off together was sunny and warm.

The Ingalsby farm and the Van Brunt farm were right next to each other, separated only by a short stone wall that had been in the same location since the land was settled. The end of that wall moved into the foothills and then up into the deep woods behind the farms. On a clear day, when the dust had settled and they were trying to remind each other why they were dating in the first place, that was where they went.

Derek spread out the blanket, and the two of them settled down, laying out their picnic of cold ham sandwiches and potato chips and preparing to eat. It was nice just to sit together and relax. And Derek needed it. He'd had enough going on in his life lately. He didn't need any more pressures.

When they were finished with the small feast, Erin lay back on the blanket and Derek looked down at her, lost quickly in the cold blue of her eyes and the way her dimples pulled at the edges of her full lips. There were times when he couldn't understand why they were together, but when he had the chance to really look at her and be with her without her friends around telling her how much better she could do, he remembered. No one on the planet understood him as well as she did, and probably no one would have put up with his temper tantrums or could make him calm down as quickly. He was working very hard at being better about it all, keeping cool, avoiding his nemesis: beer. It took time and patience. Erin was willing to give him both.

Days like this, times like this, he knew she was the girl he wanted to marry someday.

They started kissing, but something interrupted them.

At first it was just a hissing sound, like a slow leak in an old radiator, but it got louder until Derek didn't think he could ignore it, even with Erin there. He might have tried anyway, but she heard it too.

Gritting his teeth and ready to beat the crap out of any of his friends who thought they were being funny, he rolled off Erin and sat up.

The thing that stared at him wasn't even remotely human. Not a chance in hell it was a costume or anything like that. It was tall and thin, with long limbs and a rib cage woven from vines that had hardened and fused together. What little flesh seemed to cover the skeleton of vines was made of thin bark.

And the head of the thing was a revelation too. It

had a skull-like face with deep sockets, a wickedly long nose, and a half-dozen teeth that ended in jagged broken barbs.

Derek jumped up, balling his fists as the thing started moving closer, letting out a deafening screech. Erin screamed too, jumping up and pulling her sweater down. Derek took a swing at the monster, terror driving him along with the need to protect Erin. His knuckles chipped off part of its pointy jaw. It would have been hard to say whether Derek or the demon was more surprised, but the thing stopped cawing at him.

Hard wooden fingers locked onto Derek's throat, and the thing shoved him away. He grabbed the thing by its wrists and pulled, hoping to keep his balance. Instead they both tumbled down, and the freakish thing let out a caw before it tried to bite his face off.

Derek went into a full panic and started swinging, his fists hitting the misshapen head a dozen times before it released its grip on his neck and let him breathe again.

He shoved his foot into the monster's midriff and kicked as hard as he could, sending it flying. It was lighter than he'd expected, and it sailed through the air before hitting the stone fence.

It got back up again and Derek watched it, almost frozen with shock, because half of its head had broken away and it was coming at him still. The thing charged, limbs almost a blur, and he charged back, ignoring Erin's hand on his shoulder. The two of them met head-on and Derek knocked the thing flat, his body mass enough to almost guarantee that the freak was going down.

"Derek! We have to get away!"

Erin's voice was shrill with panic, and he wanted to listen, but first he had to finish it off. He pushed at the broken skull of the monster and did his best to smash it into the ground. It roared, and one of its fingers scratched a trail from his eyebrow down to the base of his chin.

Derek went a little crazy and slammed the thing's head into the ground again and again as hard as he could. The gaping wound splintered wider with each impact. His arms were already screaming from the effort, but it felt good.

Three more blows and it stopped moving. Derek looked down at the pulpy remains of its head and neck and smiled as he stood up.

He finally noticed that there was a problem when Erin screamed again.

Derek looked around and saw there were more—a lot more. At least a dozen creatures moved cautiously, eyeing him with a grudging respect.

Then three of them moved in unison, leaping at Erin. He tensed to lunge at them, ready to take them all on to defend her. But they were faster. Her short blond hair got caught in a thick hand and her head was wrenched to the side as one of the things bared wicked-looking teeth. Erin was struggling, trying to get away.

Derek swung hard and hit the thing in the face. Unlike the one he'd hit before, this one seemed heavier, more solid. The only reaction he got was a nasty grin as it lowered its head and set its teeth against Erin's bared throat. It didn't bite, but the warning burned in its eyes, telling him to back off.

Three more of the things gathered around Erin, surrounding her. There was no way he could help her as long as the freakazoid with the teeth against her neck stayed where it was. But maybe he could stop a few of the others. Derek shot out his foot like he was going to punt a football a few thousand yards and kicked at one of the things. It ducked and he staggered, fully prepared for an impact. He got several instead as they dog-piled him.

Four, five, seven, and more landed on top of Derek, their wicked hands pulling at his clothes, pinching and clawing even as the one holding Erin finally backed away from her throat and pushed her to the ground. More of them moved in, landing on top of her, but Derek was struggling to get free from the ones working him over.

Erin screamed loudly and tried to get away, but

they were all over her and all over him and he was sure they were going to die right then and there.

The sound of Erin's screams changed and Derek felt claws cutting at his clothes, tearing at them to get to his flesh. There were so many things he wanted to do, so many things he wanted to say to Erin and to his father and to, well, damned near everyone, and now it was too late.

And then the creatures jumped off him, their voices raised in a fit of cawing protests.

Something massive came out of the woods, a black form that charged faster and looked almost as big as the bull his father kept in the back west field.

Derek's heart almost stopped when he recognized the Headless Horseman. The plant things saw the Horseman too and bolted, running as fast as they could, moving on all fours in some cases and hopping like frogs in others as they let out their screaming cries and tried to get away. Even the one Derek thought he'd killed got up and started running, the remains of its head hanging loosely as it fled.

By the time Derek got back to his feet, the monsters and their pursuer were gone, lost in the forest that marked the edge of the farm.

For several seconds he stared after them, but then he looked around to find Erin. She was still on the ground, her shirt and pants as shredded as his.

Red marks covered her legs where the things had clawed her flesh.

"Erin? You okay? I think they're all gone."

Erin slapped his hand when he tried to reach for her. "You get away from me!" Her eyes blazed, and her teeth were bared as her lips pulled down into a mask of hatred.

"What? What's wrong?"

Erin sat up. "What's wrong? You bastard! Why didn't you listen to me? Why did you have to stay and fight them instead of getting away?"

"I was trying to protect you."

"Don't lie. You didn't even look at me! You just wanted to be the tough guy again; you wanted to see if you could beat one of those things!"

Derek felt all of the adrenaline in his body settle into his knees and arms, making them shake even as his stomach grew cold.

"That's not true!"

"The hell it's not! If you'd run when I told you, when I saw them coming, maybe we'd have been okay. But you think with your fists, Derek. It's always been that way. I thought maybe one of these days you'd smarten up. I've tried again and again to put up with your bullshit, but this is it. We're over."

"Erin!" he called out to her as she turned away, climbing over the low wall between their homes and stomping toward the farmhouse in the distance. She wasn't listening.

"Erin, come back! Let's talk about this!"

But then she was running, dropping her picnic basket and sailing across her front yard, moving too fast for him to even consider catching up to her. Derek stood where he was for almost ten minutes, the night growing colder and darker as he looked at the spot where he'd lost track of Erin.

Finally he gathered up his blanket and started for his house, feeling nothing at first but numb. The anger came later, after he'd washed off and changed into his sweat suit. The anger always came when he thought about how much he wanted Erin to love him. His father wasn't home either. And that didn't help.

Derek guessed he knew where his father was, but he couldn't make himself care anymore. He settled down on the porch outside his house and looked over toward Erin's home, where it sat a few fields away. He kept waiting for her to call him and apologize. He kept wanting to make the first move and call her instead. Neither one happened.

His father finally came home. He'd managed not to wreck the truck on the way, but Derek figured it was just blind luck.

God watches out for drunks and fools. That was what his old man always said. And he should know.

He was drunk and being foolish about it when Derek finally went to bed. But he stayed awake most of the night, making promises to himself that the monsters would pay for what they had done.

As parties went, it was sort of subdued. That was to be expected because, really, Alan Lancaster wasn't likely to let Shane and Aimee pull out a few beers or blast the walls of the house with a few hundred decibels of noise. But they were still having fun. The whole group was there, and Stasia had ordered enough Chinese food to feed a small army. That was good, because Hyde ate enough to feed at least a battalion just on his own.

They had been going over everything they'd learned about the tricksters, and that wasn't very much. There had been several sightings of the things in the past couple of weeks, and in most of the cases where they made themselves known, the Horseman wasn't too far behind them. The good news was that no one else had died and that none of the sightings had been on the scale of Halloween night. Just a few people, none of whom could prove what they saw. Whatever remained of the tricksters they'd destroyed on Halloween had dried up so much that it looked like nothing but vines and smashed pumpkins.

Even the news crews that had showed up on the

boot heels of Acephelos's return hadn't stayed around too long. The idea that a killer was on the loose evaporated pretty quickly since there was no film footage of the guy and no new attacks had taken place.

"So your dad is getting a little cooler about you maybe having lives again?" Jekyll was kicked back on the couch, his feet dangling off the armrest. The plate of sweet-and-sour pork resting on his stomach bobbed with each word.

Aimee thought about yelling at him but decided it could wait until he actually had an accident. She thought along the same lines every time Jekyll used himself as a place mat but so far had never actually had to start throwing fits. Jekyll was tidy; he just looked like a slob.

"He's starting to ease up a bit." She stood and started gathering plates and a few other dishes. Normally Stasia helped, but at the moment she was sitting in Shane's lap, and neither of them looked much like they wanted to move. The three of them were still coming to terms with what kinds of public displays of affection weren't going to make anyone feel awkward.

Aimee headed toward the kitchen and started rinsing dishes while the others decided what to watch next. She'd just finished when she turned around and saw Hyde standing in the doorway.

"Hey." He stepped into the kitchen and moved

closer until he was towering above her. "You haven't been very talkative. I just wanted to see if you're okay, you know, with your brother and Stasia and all of that."

Aimee looked up at him and felt herself melt just a little. He was so sweet when he wanted to be, and it always took her off guard.

"Yeah, I guess. It's still a little weird. I mean, they're good about it mostly, but seeing her in his lap takes a bit of getting used to."

Hyde got a mischievous smile on his face. "It could be worse. She could give him a lap dance. In fact, the second you left the room—"

She laughed and swatted at his bicep. "You're bad."

"Yeah, well, somebody has to be."

Aimee moved past him and got another couple of beers out of the refrigerator. Her father would have had a cow if he knew—but Aimee figured she'd take a chance. The rules were simple for the night. Dad wanted them to stay in to party, and in exchange, he wasn't allowed to come home until eleven. They still had a couple of hours before he was due home, and the evidence would be long gone by then.

She handed one to Mark and he popped it open, nodding his thanks. She opened her own and took a sip before she plunged in and told Hyde the rest of what was on her mind.

"Want to know why I'm so quiet lately?" she asked.

He nodded.

"Shane and Stasia are part of it." She paused. "So are you."

Hyde looked at her, his brows pulling together as he thought about that.

"What? I thought we were cool with our little fight a while back." He grew quiet again and seemed to mull it over. "Did I do something wrong?"

"No. Not really." She set her beer down on the counter and moved closer to him, putting her free hand on his forearm. "The thing is, I like you."

"Well, good. Because I don't like thinking I did something wrong."

He wasn't getting it. Cute, but sometimes a little dense. "No, Mark, I mean I like you. *Like you*, like you."

He stared hard at her for a second, and then he gave a soft laugh, shaking his head. "You're messing with me, right?"

Aimee's heart started kicking her in the ribs, and she bit her lower lip. She'd been so confident a second ago, and now she just felt like a moron.

"I'm sorry!" The words shot out of her mouth like rapid-fire bullets. "I just made an idiot out of myself. Just forget I ever said anything, okay? Damn. I feel so stupid." Her face felt all hot and feverish, and she wanted to run from the room but decided to try to play it cool. It would be easy, really, if she kept telling herself that and maybe had a few hundred more beers.

Hyde was looking at her like she'd grown an extra nose.

"Holy crap, Aimee, you're serious." He sounded so shocked it was almost funny.

"Just forget about it, okay? I'm sorry. I'm just a mess lately."

He didn't listen; he was busy talking too. "No, I just didn't expect to hear you say anything like that. I'm sorry. I'm a moron. Listen, we can just forget it if that's what you want. Maybe that's for the best. It's probably the beer talking anyway."

And there he was, doing it again. He was giving her an out, a way to take it all back and let her forget that she'd just told him she was into him.

Mark backed up, his face so red and embarrassed he looked like a little lost boy again and damn, he looked cute when he was doing that and there he was, going away and it was all going to be over and she'd blown her chance to let him know that she liked him and . . .

Aimee leaned up and forward and planted her lips on Mark's as hard as she could.

Mark's eyes flew wide open, and his hands moved up and grabbed her arms. In a second the surprise turned to something else as he returned the kiss. He had a strong grip, and his mouth was warm and generous, and before she could blink, she felt his tongue lash lightly at her teeth and suddenly everything felt better. That panicky butterflies-in-the-stomach feeling was washed away in a warm glow and the feeling of his body close to hers; his heartbeat pulsed even in the press of his lips to hers.

They were already against each other, and somehow he pulled her even closer, almost lifting her off her feet as the kiss kept going. It was hard to breathe, they were kissing so hard, but it was wonderful, too. She moved her hands, running them over his chest, marveling at the feel of the muscles under his battered old black T-shirt and the heat that seemed to come off him in waves.

He broke the kiss and set her down about three seconds before Jekyll came into the kitchen, carrying his plate. "Guys, is the rice in here?" By the time Steve had entered, Hyde was four feet away and running his fingers through his thick mop of hair.

Aimee looked from Hyde, red-faced and shocked, to Jekyll, who had an equally stunned expression on his face, and back again.

Hyde shot her a quick look and then turned away. "I have to go. Bye." He was out the kitchen door and on his way through the house before she could even blink.

Jekyll got a smirk on his face that she wanted to slap clean off. He was smart and didn't say a word. Aimee pushed past him into the living room just in time to see Hyde close the front door.

The echoes of the kiss were still running through her nerve endings, and she felt weak as a newborn kitten. But he was gone, and that sort of threw a whole different spin on everything. Was he pissed? Was he scared? Was he running off right now to tell Kimmie Hill that he loved her?

"This sucks. . . ."

"What?" Stasia asked. She and Shane were curled up next to each other.

Aimee rolled her eyes. "Nothing."

CHAPTER
FIVE

SHANE HAD PLANNED to get some studying done at work. Most days he could get his homework done before leaving the newspaper office. On average he could count the phone calls he received at the *Gazette* on the fingers of both hands without having to resort to counting toes. The only exception had been his first day at the newspaper, when his dad was giving the reporters and other employees a pep talk to start everything off the right way and the chaos of the Horseman's curse had been hitting the fan.

Now history was repeating itself.

He answered the phone again. "*Sleepy Hollow Gazette*, this is Shane; how can I help you?"

"There's a giant in my backyard."

Shane frowned. They might live in a town where weird stuff was becoming common, but that didn't mean there weren't still nut jobs out there. After all, a giant?

"Excuse me?"

"A giant. Well, maybe not a normal giant. He doesn't have a lot of skin."

What worried him was that she didn't sound like a nut job at all. She sounded completely sincere, though also a bit detached, as though she was in shock.

"I'm sorry, where did you say you were calling from?" The woman gave her address, and Shane wrote it down. "Have you called the police, ma'am?"

"Of course I called the police. Do I sound like an idiot to you?"

"I don't know, ma'am. We've never met." She hung up the phone, which was just as well because two other lines were ringing.

"*Sleepy Hollow Gazette*, this is Shane; how may I help you?"

"Yeah, do you know if there's supposed to be a migration of birds over the town?"

"Well, it is autumn, sir. That's when birds normally migrate."

"Oh. Yeah. Thank you."

Dial tone.

"*Sleepy Hollow Gazette*, this is Shane; how may I help you?"

"Somebody stole my rosebushes."

"Your rosebushes, ma'am?"

"Yes! My prizewinning rosebushes are all gone.

They were outside an hour ago, but they've vanished!" She sounded ready to have a heart attack.

"Did you see anyone outside before they were stolen?"

"No, they're just gone!"

"Have you called the police, ma'am?"

"Yes, and the officer I spoke to was horribly condescending. Someone knows something, though, I'm sure of that. I want to place an ad, young man. I want to post a reward for my rosebushes."

"I'll connect you to the advertising department; one moment, please." He put her on hold and called out for Professor Bisby to answer line four. Far back in the bull pen of the office, Bisby raised a hand to signal that he'd heard and picked up the phone.

By then Shane was already on to the next call. "*Sleepy Hollow Gazette*, this is Shane; how can I help you?"

"Shane? Oh, wow, I didn't expect you to answer!"

"I'm sorry, who's this?"

"Oh. This is Alicia D'Agostino. I just thought . . ." Her voice trailed off. She sounded nervous and afraid.

"Alicia? What is it? What's wrong?"

"I . . . I just . . . well, I heard that you keep track of this stuff, the weird stuff, and I thought you might want to know that the tree is back. The Whispering Tree."

"Really? You've seen it?" His pulse quickened.

That damned tree was on his list of monsters to wipe out, but it had vanished a while back.

"No, but I think I heard it last night."

"Where?"

"In my backyard; the tree stole my mother's rose-bushes. She's totally pissed."

Shane blinked. "That's two rosebush thefts in one day. Weird."

"That is weird. What would somebody want with all those roses?"

"Maybe some guy really, really needs to make up for doing something stupid. Anyway, I gotta go, Alicia. The phones are going crazy today. Thanks for calling."

"Okay, bye, sweetie!"

He hung up, wondering when, exactly, he had become a sweetie.

"*Sleepy Hollow Gazette*, this is Shane; how may I help you?"

"Yeah, it's me again. Do birds normally drop out of the sky and fall all over Main Street when they're migrating?"

"Um . . . no, sir, I don't think they do."

"Well, they do now. Looks like a hundred, maybe a hundred and fifty birds. I'm looking right now, and they're all over the street, and there's maybe fifteen cars all bumped into each other."

"Where on Main Street are you, sir?" He spun around in his chair and waved to his father, who came out of his office, brow furrowed in curiosity, as Shane wrote down the address.

"Thank you for calling."

Alan took up the stack of messages Shane had written down and flipped through them, and his expression darkened. He glanced at the most recent one, about dying birds and a multicar accident, and nodded, already heading for his coat. Shane walked away from the desk for the ten seconds it took to make sure his father took the cell phone with him this time.

"Sun's going down soon. Here's the money for a cab." His father dropped thirty dollars in front of him. It wouldn't cost anywhere near that much, and Shane knew it.

"I want you and Aimee home tonight when I get back. I think we need to talk."

"Okay. I don't think either of us had plans anyway. Aimee's working."

"Damn, I forgot about that. Well, you should have enough to pick her up from the theater, too."

Just as Alan was heading for the door, Ed Burroughs pushed in, scowling even more than he usually did, his face pale and sallow.

"Alan, can we talk?"

"Yeah, Ed, of course."

Burroughs started heading for Alan's office, and Shane's father grimaced and went with him. The birds would have to wait. The radio at the chief's hip was crackling with tense voices. The cops must be having as much fun as Shane was.

He answered the phone again, barely willing to pay attention. "*Sleepy Hollow Gazette*, this is Shane; how may I help you?"

"I was just attacked by a shrub!"

"I'm sorry, one more time, please?"

"A shrub! A shrub tried to eat my face!"

That one he could relate to, sort of. "Can I get your address?" He wrote and listened as much as he had to, but mostly he focused on Ed Burroughs and his father back in the office as the two men talked. The police chief was a wreck, and it showed. His job was on the line. His record as a police officer and as the leader of the department was dependent on getting the job done daily, and ever since the Headless Horseman had come back to town, Shane knew the mayor of Sleepy Hollow was breathing fire and snorting steam when it came to Burroughs.

A few minutes later, as the phones continued to ring, the police chief left the building with Alan right behind him.

The phone rang.

"*Sleepy Hollow Gazette*, this is Shane; how may I help you?"

Nightfall came over the cemetery in quick waves as the sun set behind the hills. Before they had even reached the markers, Ella Cairns knew that they would be leaving in near-perfect darkness.

Still, it was tradition. Every month they made the trip to see the family, and this late in the year they always ended up leaving after the sun was down. It was a good thing her grandmother was something of a local celebrity with the groundskeepers. The cemetery closed promptly at four thirty in the afternoon, and normally no one was allowed to stay later than that. Wilhelmina Cairns was an energetic old woman and one of the sweetest people walking the earth. She was the only person Ella had ever met for whom the rules could nearly always be changed.

Which was good, because as spry as her grandmother was, the autumnal weather changes were playing havoc on her arthritis, and she was moving slowly. They'd parked the car near the top of the hill, and now they had to walk the remaining distance. Her cousins were there, though, and Jacob was a big guy, large enough to carry Nana all the way back to the car if he had to. It had never come to that, thank goodness.

They stood in front of the family plot for several minutes, Wilhelmina carefully wiping down the headstones and the cousins placing fresh wreaths while Ella removed the few pieces of debris that had fallen in the area. They stayed until, as she had predicted, the sun had gone down.

So the sudden flare of sunrise to the north confused them.

"Is that a fire over there?" her cousin Mitch said, almost dreamily. Mitch wasn't the quickest.

Ella was about to tease him, a favorite pastime among the Cairns cousins, but then the smell reached her. It took her a moment to realize it wasn't smoke. Something was coming their way from where the light was blazing, and it stank like hell. The first thing that came to mind was a dead skunk on the side of the road.

The light blazed brighter, and Ella moved in that direction, worried.

She was the first person to see it clearly.

The ground north of her family plot was shaking, graves rupturing as decayed flesh and bone split the soil and the lawn, rising up to spiral in midair. Entire corpses and fragments of dead matter were caught in a web of light and reeled toward the thing standing in the center of the cemetery.

It was thin and misshapen. One arm was longer than the other, and the legs of the creature were different widths and shapes. The thing stood with its oversized head bowed and its arms held wide apart as the bodies buried in the Old Dutch Settlers Cemetery slithered through the air and melded to its deformed shape. Already it was at least twelve feet tall, and she could see that the withered flesh and bone rising from the graves was only adding to its size.

Terror suffused Ella, and she felt a rush of blood through her that warmed her with her own fear, making the icy chill racing down her back all the colder. Her heart hammered in her chest and her throat closed up, causing her to gasp for breath. For the first time in her life she understood what it really was to be afraid.

She could barely make out any of the monster's features through the illumination that limned its form, but the one impression she had that scared her most was that the thing was still only an infant. A baby, really.

No. Close, but not quite a baby. It was even more unsettling than that.

It was something being born.

It started to lift its massive head and Ella stepped back, terrified that it might see her. She ran back to her family and didn't bother with any sort of excuse. "We're leaving. Right now."

One look at the expression on her face was enough to get them moving.

"What did you see, Ella, honey?" Wilhelmina asked.

"Nothing you need to know about, Nana. But we've got to go."

She dodged around a headstone and took her

grandmother's arm. Her small herd of cousins was right behind them. Whatever the thing was, it had started moving after them, cutting through a ridge of trees, knocking them down as it came. Ella pulled out her cell phone and started punching in numbers.

Alan and the chief had returned to the office, and Shane hadn't had a chance to leave yet. It was well past dark now, but the phone calls kept coming in.

His father looked at him and said, "It's enough, Shane. Put on the answering machine."

Shane nodded, but before he could turn the machine on, another call came in. "*Sleepy Hollow Gazette*, this is Shane; how can I help you?"

"Shane?" a woman's voice said, edgy and frantic. "This is Ella Cairns; is your father there?"

"Yeah, hang on a second, Ella." He looked to his father and nodded. "Line three is for you. Ella Cairns. She sounds freaked."

His father grabbed up the phone and had barely gotten out a hello before he shut his mouth and started listening. The expression on his face said it wasn't good. He asked a few questions, jotted some notes, then hung up the phone and shot a look at Chief Burroughs.

"We have a situation at the Old Dutch. Ella Cairns and her family are there, and they're being chased by something. Something big."

Burroughs frowned. "Okay. Did she call the station?"

"She did," Alan replied without meeting the man's gaze. "They thought she was just another kook. Sleepy Hollow PD's been getting a lot of strange calls tonight."

Burroughs nodded grimly. "We'll take my car."

Alan shook his head. "You lead, sirens and all. I'll follow. Grab your coat, Shane. Let's go."

While Shane was grabbing his things and locking up the office, Alan walked outside with the chief. The minute they were on the sidewalk, Burroughs shot him a hard look.

"Are you sure about taking your boy along?"

"Yes. You might say he's becoming something of an expert in this sort of thing."

Burroughs tilted his head, eyes narrowed. "Want to explain that?"

"Later. After we get to Ella."

He'd never heard her sound so scared, not even when the things in her theater had almost managed to ruin its grand opening beyond repair and people were running everywhere.

"Damn right we will," the chief said.

Shane came up behind them; Burroughs gave him a doubtful look and then got into his car. Alan got into his own car and started it up as Shane climbed into the passenger seat. If he'd heard any of the conversation Alan had had with Burroughs, he said nothing.

Alan followed Burroughs down the road at high speed. The sirens and flashers ripped through the night, and Alan was hard-pressed to keep up. They were at the gates of the Old Dutch in a matter of minutes, and the groundskeeper opened them as the police squad car came forward.

The place was huge, rolling hills lined with narrow paths, some paved and some dirt and gravel, that wound amid headstones and crypts and tombs built into the hillside. There were ridges lined with trees, and down in the valley to their right, which was littered with granite and marble grave markers, the cemetery bumped right up to the woods. Alan hadn't bothered going into the Old Dutch before but realized almost immediately that they were going to have trouble finding out where Ella and her family were.

The cruiser came to a stop when they reached a parked van that completely blocked the way. Alan had barely parked the car before Shane was out of his seat and pointing to an area off to their left, where light was shimmering in the darkness like a beacon.

Half a second behind his son, Alan heard the screams coming from that direction. All three men ran hard, and Alan hoped they were prepared for what lay ahead of them.

"There they are!" Shane shouted, and he put on more speed, legs pumping beneath him. Ella Cairns was moving toward them, her arm around the older woman he knew as Willie. There were four other people behind them, each looking about ready to have a coronary. Wilhelmina Cairns was pasty white, and her breathing was labored.

When Shane saw what was moving just beyond them, he could understand the sudden chest pains. The thing seemed to be growing right out of the ravaged earth of the graveyard, but Shane could see that the appearance was deceptive. It was freed from the ground and walking toward them, even as the graves throughout the cemetery erupted, spilling thick sod out of the way and releasing the corpses that rested underneath. Parts of the dead people were being suctioned toward the giant like iron filings to a magnet, and they were sticking to the thing as it grew and changed.

It wasn't ten feet tall.

More like fifteen, and still growing.

Ed Burroughs said, "You've gotta be kidding me." His voice broke like a freshman's.

Shane's father was wordier and far more profane. He ran toward Shane and joined up with him as they finally reached Ella and her family. Shane took one of Willie's arms and Alan took the other.

"Alan, what the hell is that thing?" Ella pleaded.

He shook his head. "I don't have answers. All I know is, you're not moving fast enough."

"Jacob," Ella said, turning to her cousin. "Carry Nana."

Willie's grandson picked her up even as she let out a squeak of protest.

The ground was fairly even, and they made fast progress. The demon, or whatever the hell it was chasing them, let out an incoherent growl and moved after them faster than before, a shambling tower of rotted flesh and jutting, moonlit bone. They had a small advantage but only because the damned thing wasn't well balanced. It was growing, yes, but it wasn't an even progression, and the weight it carried as it moved kept changing.

Ed Burroughs was in front of them. He hadn't even made it as far as Ella and her family on the way. Once he'd caught sight of the thing, the chief had frozen in place. Shane's eyes burned and his hands shook a little when he let the image of the thing sear into his mind, and he thought about the dead, all those graves of the dead, torn up and their bones drawn together to form this thing. It made him sick.

So he understood Burroughs's horror and his

fear. As they ran past him, the chief just stood staring at the thing coming their way.

Alan called out, "Ed! Come on, man. We've got to get these people out of here."

The police chief looked around and nodded, shaking himself out of his stupor.

"You go! I've got your backs!" Burroughs shouted.

Shane risked a quick look over his shoulder to see the man drawing his revolver.

Wilhelmina Cairns was making a nervous whining sound in the back of her throat. They finally got back to the cars, and Jacob set the elderly woman down against the side of the squad car. Ella held her in place while she caught her breath. Shane looked back the way they had just come but didn't see Chief Burroughs. Then the gunshots started echoing off the grave markers around them. And the screams too.

Shane had never heard any man scream that way.

He turned and ran, moving toward the sound as fast as he could, ignoring his father's shouts for him to stop.

Ed Burroughs looked at the nightmare coming his way and almost lost it again. There was no space in his world for monsters. He'd heard all the rumors going around but had never let himself believe a word.

Now his breath came in hitching gasps and he

stared at the thing, shaking his head. He'd come up with ways to explain away all of the stories he'd heard . . . but this was no story, and it wasn't going away.

His heart hammered in his chest and he couldn't breathe. His legs felt like they were made of lead, and as he raised his pistol, his hands shook. The thing came closer, and Burroughs took careful aim. It sensed something, for it looked his way, letting him see its face for the first time. The head was cloaked in a kind of shifting shadow. Even with light streaming around the giant, its features remained in darkness. But he could make out a powerful jawline that almost seemed more like it belonged on a carnivore than a human being, and he could see the dual slits of its nostrils as they flared with each breath it drew. A thick flap of flesh covered the single massive socket where its eye must have hidden.

Only one eye? No. It looked like a second eye was there as well but dwarfed by the larger one, the one that had grown and swollen inside the thing's head until it was large enough to cover a third of the entire skull.

One massive leg moved forward, kicking over a headstone in the shape of an angel looking toward the heavens. The marble broke into small fragments and scattered across the ground.

Enough. Burroughs pulled the trigger and fired at

the monster. The bullet tore into the creature's torso and blew out the back. The eerie lights that had bathed the thing since it showed up suddenly winked out, and it let out a deep moan that became a threatening rumble. The thing stopped in its tracks and swayed for a second, then started forward even faster, reaching for him. It moved too quickly, got too close.

Burroughs fired again and again and again until the bullets stopped blazing and he heard repeated clicks as the chambers spun in the revolver. The head turned toward him and the massive eyelid rose, revealing the sickening, pustulant eye hidden beneath it.

He screamed as their eyes met.

Alan ran as fast as he could, worried far more about his son than about the painful stitch he'd developed in his side. He felt fear unlike anything he'd ever known, bone deep and primal, clutching at his insides. But Shane, the shy boy who seldom argued with him, was running back to where the monster was, seeking to help a man Alan knew his son didn't like very much. And no matter how ancient and powerful the fear in him was, Alan never hesitated for a moment. If it cost his life to save Shane's, that was more than a fair trade.

A long, agonized shriek split the night as the

world up ahead grew as bright as noon. He saw Shane cover his face and drop to the ground, looking away from the source of the light. Alan, a little farther back but in perfect line of sight, saw everything that happened with horrifying clarity.

Ed Burroughs looked up at the giant that was growing larger every moment. The man's broad, rugged face showed all the fear he should have been experiencing, but there was anger there, too. Then the monster's eye came into view, a huge, bloated thing that had been hidden and now showed itself in all its terrifying glory. It didn't even look fully formed in the head of the beast, but it vomited light into the night and poured that glow over Ed Burroughs.

The chief looked directly into that light, and all the doubt and anger left his face, replaced instantly by raw terror and pain. Where the light touched his flesh, he was instantly burned. Skin blackened and smoked and split open under the power of that gaze, and the man's hair went from steely gray to stark bleached white even as he threw his arms up to shield himself.

Ed's scream seemed to go on long after he was dead, but that might have just been Alan trying to absorb what he had seen.

It wasn't heat that boiled the man alive, but it was definitely power. Alan felt the blazing energies that came from the massive cyclopean orb even from fifty yards away, and he could only imagine the agony of being bathed in that searing light.

The blackened ash and bone that had been Ed Burroughs fell to the ground as the creature looked away, its eyelid once again falling to cover the uneven iris and pupil.

And now it wasn't Ed who was screaming. Alan realized that even as the world went black for him. It was Shane. His son moved forward, running to the fallen man even as the giant turned away. He reached Burroughs's side and fell next to the charred remains in the grass, a shadow falling beside a silhouette.

Alan moved as fast as he could, worried that his son had been scorched by the monster's gaze.

Shane was fine; he realized that as the afterimage of the light slowly faded. Shane was staring down at the wreckage of Ed Burroughs's body, eyes locked on the ruined face, its features stuck for all time in a frozen silent scream, and at the blown-out sockets where the man's eyes should have been.

CHAPTER
SIX

LARRY WINTERS WAS nervous but excited. He was
going hunting again, and this time he was doing it
with a few buddies. Normally, during the hunting
season in New York, he didn't have too much spare
time. If school wasn't getting in the way, his father
was. Not that his father was opposed to hunting. As
far as his father was concerned, until Larry's grades
got better, he wasn't allowed to have a social life.
That was the main reason he had been forced to
move back home: a little slip in his grades and suddenly all the fun was sucked from the day.

So this time he and Kevin and Brian and Dean
forgot to mention that they were heading out of
Tarrytown and into the woods around Sleepy Hollow.
He told his father he was getting together with his
buddies from the university for a cram session, and
the old man believed him. The best truth came out in
lies. Classes were almost done, and he did need to
study for finals, but one night off with his friends

would do him a world of good for relaxing.

Dean was driving, so he avoided the beer for now. Larry didn't feel the need to follow that little rule and pulled one from the first case. Kevin and Brian joined him.

Brian knocked back most of his Budweiser in one long gulp and then belched loudly enough to be heard over the booming sounds of classic Beastie Boys on the radio. Dean laughed and so did the other two; Larry thought it was disgusting, but he laughed anyway.

Dean pulled his Jeep off the road and they climbed out, shocked by the bitter cold in the air. It seemed like it was five times colder in the woods than it had been on campus, but Larry always felt that way. The woods around Sleepy Hollow were just like that.

"Come on! Let's go shoot us a Sasquatch!" Kevin was just about jumping up and down. He was the one who'd come up with the idea in the first place, and he was pumped about hunting down anything that didn't look like natural flora or fauna. So many people were talking about weird stuff all over town that the word had gotten around. Kevin had dragged them out to hunt. He wasn't in it for the sport; Kevin wanted to be famous. And if he couldn't decide what they were hunting, no one really cared. They were just along for the fun.

Larry let out a howl and grabbed his 12-gauge. He intended to shoot the Horseman full of buckshot and take pictures with the corpse. Even if there really was a living person inside a costume—and he didn't think there was, because he'd been there on Halloween night when the Horseman had ridden up Main Street, and that had been one scary thing to see—they'd still be heroes.

All of them were ready for a good time.

They stayed ready, too, right up until Brian let out a scream and jumped half out of his own skin.

Dean laughed. "What's the matter, McPherson? You see a ghost?"

Brian didn't answer. He was too busy staring into the dark of the woods, and suddenly not even Dean seemed to think it was funny.

They looked around, trying to spot what it was that had Brian so jumpy. Larry carefully switched the safety to the off position on his shotgun and scanned the spaces between the trees, the hairs on his neck standing up.

He said, "Brian, dude, if this is a joke, I'm gonna shoot you myself."

"Not joking, Lar . . . Look up and to the right, on the branches."

He did. He scanned several tree limbs before he saw what the big deal was. The thing that was crouched up there stared back down at him, its long, thin face spreading into a vile-looking smile and a deep red gleam lighting its eyes.

"What the hell is that thing?" Kevin's voice was suddenly subdued.

Dean let out a little laugh. "Which one?"

They came down from the trees in a wave, skittering like bugs, all long limbs and liquid, flowing movements. Some were at ground level, and many more were hidden among the branches. Larry let out a shriek and dropped his shotgun, absolutely terrified as they kept coming. There seemed to be hundreds.

Dean was faster on the draw. He managed to swing his rifle around and take aim before the creatures were all over them. He never pulled the trigger, though. They'd torn out his throat before his finger found it.

Larry let out several more screams before they were done. He begged for mercy. No one came to save him, and the tricksters were not merciful.

It was cold out, and neither David Hendricks nor Nick Montrose wanted anything to do with being outside. Unfortunately for them, their job required it. Something big and clumsy had knocked down half the phone lines on Perry Avenue, and they were the ones who had to put them back up.

Hendricks scratched at the small of his back and

then put his wrench to work, torquing the thin metallic fasteners around the heavy cable. "Done over here, Nick! How's on your side?"

"Gimme a minute, Davy! This bitch is putting up a fight!"

"Don't take too long! The first beer's on me."

Nick laughed. "Yeah, that *would* be a first."

Dave shrugged as he put away his tools. "I got lucky last night at poker. You get done in the next ten, I'll even make it two beers and a bowl of LeAnne's chowder."

Nick went into overdrive. As cold as they both were, chowder sounded like paradise.

Dave stretched and rolled his shoulders, loosening some of the tension that had locked up his muscles. He closed his eyes and thought about bed. Their shift had officially been over almost two hours ago, but they couldn't just leave the work unfinished if they wanted to keep their jobs.

When he opened his eyes again, something new had been added. A thing was looking at him, its face almost at eye level. That wouldn't have been so bad, but currently he was on top of a cherry picker and his eye level was eighteen feet off the ground.

"What the hell!" Dave stepped back as far as he could, the entire basket he stood in rocking dangerously. He was too shocked to be scared.

The thing moved closer to him now, its massive,

misshapen skull almost as big as his own body. He could make out one tiny eye next to a giant cancerous-looking bulge that made up a third of the thing's head.

Dave stared at the thing and tried to will himself somewhere, anywhere else in the whole world.

Off to his right the other cherry picker started down, lowering Nick, and the thing looked away from Dave for a second, its single minuscule eye tracking what Nick was doing. The monster looked like it was made entirely of rotting flesh. Bare bone showed through in places, and it stank of death.

Dave whimpered. Aside from the weird lump and the tiny eye next to it, the creature had a face that made him think of a bat. Thick slits of flesh curled around the center of the face where a nose should have been. And below that a wide mouth with thin lips that still seemed unformed twitched with the promise of a snarl.

A neck as thick as Dave's whole body supported the massive head, and the thing's body looked like it belonged on a gigantic gorilla. It was heavy with muscle, some of which was exposed. Veins and arteries were also visible, running along the outside of its twisted flesh, and they pulsed with each beat of the thing's heart. Bone even showed through in places.

Nick had finally seen the thing . . . and hadn't run. The fool was in the street, waving his arms and jumping around like a chimpanzee, trying to get its attention. He had it. The monster took one step toward him.

"Nick! You run, man! You run and you get help!"

"What? No way! I'm not leaving you out here alone!"

Dave was about to answer, to tell him to just call the damned cops already, but before he could, the cancerous-looking thing on the monster's head opened up. What he'd thought was just a thick fold in the growth tore open, revealing a bulging red mass of an eye. At first it seemed to have no iris, no pupil, but as Dave watched, speechless again and frozen with fear, the black pit of a pupil rolled into view, sliding down from apparently staring at the inside of the monster's skull and then focusing on poor, stubborn Nick.

Nick started to scream, to protect himself from the stark white glow that erupted from that gargantuan eye. His hands lifted, but they slowed as they rose until he was as stiff as if he were made of stone. His skin split like hard-baked mud, spilling a heavy flow of blood that soaked his clothes in an instant.

Dave looked on, frozen, until the very end, when Nick simply fell apart, breaking like fine porcelain as he hit the ground. Even his eyes, always smiling on the worst days, shattered.

And then the thing was turning and looking toward Dave. Dave stared into the quivering pupil of the massive eye for the last few seconds of his life.

Even when his eyes exploded, his mind kept staring at the memory of what he saw.

Aimee gazed at the mass of people as they spilled into the church, numb to their presence. They were just there; they didn't really matter. What mattered was that it had happened again. Someone she knew was dead. She might not have liked Chief Burroughs much, and the feeling had been mutual, but no one should have to die the way he had.

It was obvious that her father was feeling a lot of guilt about the man's death. So was Shane. Both of them had been at the cemetery when he was murdered. Both of them had seen the thing that had killed him with just a look. Neither of them could have stopped it, but they seemed to think they should have managed it anyway.

It was the death of Ed Burroughs that was keeping them in Sleepy Hollow. She knew that. Just the night before, their father had sat them down for a talk. Aimee and Shane had both expected him to say they were moving. They'd been ready to argue tooth and nail and to go into the fight with everything they had, because someone had to believe in the darkness, had to do something about it. And it was their responsibility, even if their father didn't see it that way.

"Before we talk about what you really want to talk about," he had said, "there's something I want to know. Ichabod Crane . . . if there really was such a person and he was some kind of, what, sorcerer or something, how did things get so out of control?"

Shane had spoken first. "Right, well, forget the 'if's. He was real, and he was Mom's ancestor and ours. We told you we found the family crypt. We've done the research."

Their dad had nodded. "Okay, I'll go with you on that." He sounded dubious.

Shane continued. "Near as we've been able to figure, he *was* a sorcerer. Just not a very good one. When he came to Sleepy Hollow, he made a deal with the town's founders. He promised them prosperity if they let him have a say in what happened. We think he was trying to use sympathetic magic. He wanted to make it rain, he tried to summon rain spirits. Only he wasn't doing it right. Whatever he summoned to do his bidding stayed around. And he just ignored them. But things were getting ugly, and he couldn't ignore them for long. Even with crops prospering and all, it was getting sort of crowded here in the monster department. The town council ordered him to fix the situation."

Alan stared at them. "And how did you find out about all this in the first place?"

Shane hesitated, so Aimee had said what they were both thinking.

"A ghost told us. One of Stasia's ancestors."

Their father held his head in his hands for a moment and then chuckled. "All right. Given what I've seen and what you've told me, I should be able to process that. A ghost."

"And we've told you the rest," Aimee said. "He had to find a powerful demon to stop the other monsters, something tough enough to drive them all away or keep them in check. What he found was Acephelos. Crane was supposed to sacrifice himself, give up his body, so Acephelos—a headless demon out of ancient myth—could manifest in our world, but he cheated and gave up his friend instead. Then he got out of town. The town council made their bargain with the Horseman, the pact trading his services for Crane's blood if he or his descendants ever returned to the Hollow. He agreed and everything was fine until we moved here."

Alan nodded. "Right, right. This part you've explained." He paused and regarded first Aimee and then Shane. She knew what was coming, knew there was no way he would consider staying in town.

"I was ready to leave, guys. I had planned to tell you that the night Ed died. And after seeing that thing in the cemetery, I was pretty sure I was making the right choice. But I got to thinking, and I realized you're right. If I just left . . . the people would be on their own, with no one to tell them what to watch out for. I don't know if I could live with myself, abandoning the town like that. So we're going to try this for a while. If you still want to and you can live with the rules we've established."

They had talked about the details for a while, and it boiled down to letting him know everything so that maybe he could let the police know what they were looking for. How well that would go was uncertain, because no one knew yet who the new police chief would be. When they'd had their conversation, Ed Burroughs hadn't even been buried yet.

The church service was over. The pallbearers walked to the coffin and lifted it, and everyone watched in silence as they carried the earthly remains of police chief Edgar R. Burroughs along the aisle and out the front doors, the priest leading with a censer of incense and a procession of cops following, heads lowered in respect and mourning.

At the graveside service the mayor spoke of the chief's commitment to preserving the peace and his dedication to his job. Shane stood on the sidelines, watching the somber-faced police officers lower the Burroughs into the ground. Aimee was taking it badly, and so was Stasia. Jekyll barely moved or made a gesture, and Hyde was as glum as ever. There'd been no love lost between Hyde and Burroughs. Shane was a little surprised to see him there. Then again, half of the school seemed to be present.

Aimee was trembling, and their father put his hands over her shoulders, pulling her close. Dad just looked confused, which was exactly how Shane felt. The Horseman was bad, and the naiads had been beautiful but deadly. The gremlins were unsettling and had left him angry with himself because, really, in the end, he almost felt sorry for what he and his friends had been forced to do. The Whispering Tree was freaky, and the harvest spirits were right up there on his list of things he didn't like to think too much about. But the giant from the other night? That one wasn't leaving him alone. He'd looked away before he got too good a look at the monstrous eye of the thing when it opened. Call it instinct or whatever, he'd had the good sense not to stare. But even the brief peek he'd gotten had been enough to scare the hell out of him.

Not since his first glimpse of the Horseman had he felt such terror. And maybe not even then, not primal and bone deep like this.

He made himself look down as the casket was lowered into the ground. Ed Burroughs was dead, and nothing he did could change that. Stasia slid up next to him and leaned into his shoulder. He took a lot of comfort from her, but his mind was still working over everything that was happening in Sleepy Hollow even as the dirt fell on the top of Ed Burroughs's casket.

CHAPTER
SEVEN

DEREK VAN BRUNT was not having a good week. Today it was roses: they'd cost more than he wanted to think about, but he figured the expense was acceptable if he could just win Erin back. He was miserable without her.

He'd spent most of the last week doing everything he could think of to change his girlfriend's mind about splitting up with him, but so far he was batting zero. Every time he'd screwed up in the past, she'd finally let him back into her heart, but this time nothing was working.

Still, he had to try. So he knocked on her door and waited patiently to see who would answer. If it was her mother, he had a chance. If it was her father, it was time to start back across the field and head for home. Jim Ingalsby was being a bastard about the whole thing.

It was Erin. Her face didn't exactly light up with joy when she saw him.

"We don't have anything to talk about, Derek."

"Erin, please don't be like this." Ugh, he sounded like he was whining. He hated that.

"Be what way? Sane?" Her voice was harsh and bordered on laughter. Hearing her tone was enough to make him want to scream.

"Erin, I was trying to protect you."

"No, you weren't. You were being a tough-guy jerk!" Her eyes flashed and she leaned toward him, all of her pretty features ruined by her anger. "You were trying to prove you weren't afraid or something, when any normal person would have known there's a time to fight and a time to run, and that was the time to run, Derek! If the Horseman hadn't shown up . . . Look, the key thing here is that you didn't even turn and look at me when I called for help. I'm sick of it, Derek. Sick of whatever it is inside you that makes you have to have your fists up all the time. All you ever do is pick on guys like Shane Lancaster or on your special days slap a girl like Aimee across the face because she tells the truth."

Ouch. He couldn't argue with that. "I was drunk and being stupid."

"How is that a defense? You've been drunk and stupid for almost as long as we've been dating." She started talking with her hands, emphasizing everything she said with wild gestures. That was never, ever a good sign with Erin.

"I haven't had anything to drink in over a week now."

"Did you even consider apologizing to Stasia? You did everything you could to call her out as a slut at that party."

"She's the one going out with every guy on the planet." He muttered the words and regretted them as soon as he realized Erin had heard him.

When she spoke again, the temperature around her seemed to drop at least fifteen degrees. "No. Like you pointed out, she's going out with Shane. Which just kills you because she's not going out with you."

"Erin, come on . . ."

"Go home, Derek. There's nothing left to say. You already made it clear who you want to be with." Her eyes were blinking furiously, but she didn't actually let any tears flow as she turned away and went back inside.

Derek dropped the roses on the porch and walked away. He wasn't strutting like he normally did. He couldn't think of a single reason to be cocky.

He'd just climbed over the low wall between the properties when he caught sight of them from the corner of his eye. Two of the freaks were at the edge of the woods, their backs turned to him. A tiny ripple of fear went through him, and then it was plowed under by hatred. If it wasn't for those things screwing with him, Erin wouldn't be pissed at him right now. Without even thinking, he crouched low and moved for his backyard, his temper starting a fast climb toward pissed off.

His baseball bat was exactly where he'd left it the day before, and he snatched it up before returning to the stone wall. They were still where he'd seen them before, crouched low and working on something. He didn't care what they were doing as long as they kept looking the other way.

The things that were squatting at the edge of his family's property owed Derek a week's worth of misery, and he intended to collect. He stayed low and moved along the wall until he was only a few feet from them. They were speaking to each other, just chatting away in whatever passed for a language between them.

Derek didn't announce his presence. He just came up swinging. The baseball bat clocked one of the creatures on the back of the head and sent it falling forward. He hit it again, the vibrations running through the bat and jarring his hands with the impact. For the moment at least, the weird-looking plant thing stayed down.

The other one did not. It reared back when Derek popped up from behind the wall, and then it let out a screech and leaped for him. Derek wasn't quite fast enough to block the thing when it came for him, but he deflected its attack enough that instead of ripping into his face, its claws struck his shoulder and cut into his jacket.

Derek kicked out at the thing as it tried to climb on top of him and sent it stumbling backward, only to trip over its fallen brethren. Before it could regain its footing, he attacked again, brought the bat down with all of the savagery he could manage, grunting with each impact. Rage was boiling inside him, and it felt good to cut loose.

The bat dented the creature's face with the first blow and shattered its temple with the second. Before he could hit it a third time, it was calling out with that weird crowlike laughter, and Derek heard several of the things answering from the woods.

He also heard something else: a deep rumbling sound that shook the ground beneath his feet. Derek prepared to swing again, but both of the things backed away from him, Cheshire cat smiles on their warped faces. He was just angry enough to think they were going to run from him, so Derek went after them, bat at the ready and muscles tensed to knock their heads into the next month.

Then he saw the giant, and the bat dropped from his fingers. He stared up at the misshapen, gruesome face of the monster and froze, terrified. He was still staring when the eye of the beast opened and stared back.

Derek's screams echoed through the woods behind his family farm. No one but the creatures around him heard the sounds.

Erin Ingalsby had a dream about Derek that night. In the dream he was drunk and in his forties and they were married. They had three children, all of whom lived in fear of Daddy coming home smelling of beer. It was one of the dreams where she wasn't really sure if she was fully asleep when she had it or just thought about the idea too hard when she was drifting into unconsciousness.

She was sure that what she and Derek had was love. They had been friends for as long as either could remember, and later they'd become more than friends. He was a perfect fit for her when he was sober and not being an ass about everything.

But she was just as sure that she hated him now and then. She hated how he acted when he was drinking and when he got jealous of her even looking at another guy. She hated when he decided to make himself feel better by belittling someone else, and she hated when he ignored her because he was feeling a little too macho for his own good.

And at last she had forced herself to realize that the bad in him outweighed the good. That was why she'd broken up with him. When he was being the Derek she loved, it wasn't that she was seeing his true self, it was that he was trying to prove himself to her.

No, that wasn't even it, really. It wasn't *her* he was always trying to prove something to; it was *himself*.

She was up with the sunrise, the same as she was every day, and Erin pulled on her clothes from the day before so she could go out to the chicken coop and gather the eggs. Her parents were very understanding about her priorities. They let her have her time in school and for cheerleading and even for the occasional party. But she still had to do a few chores around the farm, end of discussion. Gathering the eggs was one of her duties.

The Ingalsby farm wasn't fully automated, and they didn't have thousands of chickens. They had a couple dozen. It was enough for their needs and to sell a few eggs to a neighboring farm whose owner did the whole farmer's market routine every day. All she had to do was grab the eggs and not get clawed to death by the chickens in the process. Then she fed the crazy birds, and she could come back in and take her shower and get ready for school.

School. Where she'd have to see Derek. All she wanted to do was crawl back into her bed for a week or so and try not to think about him.

Then she opened her front door, and that became impossible in the last way she ever could have expected.

Erin opened her mouth to scream at the sight that greeted her, but no sound came out. Derek was just lying there on the porch, apparently awake but staring blankly upward. His mouth was partially open and leaving a gathering puddle of drool on the floorboards beneath him. His clothes were soiled, covered in dirt and stained with something she didn't even want to think about.

And his hair, his perfect, wonderful blond hair, had changed color. It was no longer the color of wheat at sunset but of snow at high noon—stark white.

Erin couldn't speak or think. She stared at Derek for almost a full minute, barely moving, holding her breath most of that time while she looked for some sign that what she was looking at was truly alive.

Then she reached down and touched his face. He was warm. Breathing.

"Derek," she whispered, and then she ran inside to find her father.

After that her day became a blur of phone calls and long waits before anyone would tell her what she had already begun to fear.

Derek Van Brunt's body was alive and well, but his mind was gone.

The star of the football team had lost his marbles, as Hyde so affectionately put it. But even he said the words with more confusion and dread than humor. For no reason that anyone knew, Derek Van Brunt was in a catatonic state. He was currently in the hospital, where they were examining him for every imaginable type of toxin.

Shane didn't think they'd find anything. Neither did Stasia, who'd taken the news harder than he'd expected. Once upon a time she and Derek had been friends and possibly more. She had never really said, and he didn't want to ask. He understood that there were things he didn't know and probably never would.

They were sitting in the Muffin Man: him and Stasia and Hyde and Jekyll and Aimee. None of them was speaking very much. There was a part of Shane that wanted to feel guilty for cleaning Derek's clock, but it was a small part, and he chose to ignore it. Derek had dogged him since the Lancasters had moved to Sleepy Hollow. He'd been such a bastard that Shane couldn't feel too bad about the fight. But he was still getting chills about the fact that Van Brunt had lost his mind overnight.

Aimee sighed and reached for her coffee. "Well, this sucks."

Stasia just nodded and looked into her own cup as if trying to divine some secret answer to everything going on.

Hyde looked at Aimee for a few seconds and

then glanced at his watch. "Gotta go to work. Later." He left quickly, his normal brooding expression hiding whatever he might have felt about Derek.

Jekyll watched him go, brow furrowed with concern, and then stole what was left of Hyde's chocolate milk shake. He drank it fast enough to half freeze his eyeballs and then waved goodbye, leaving the table almost as quickly as Hyde.

When they were both gone, Shane turned to the girls. "What the hell got into them?"

"What do you mean?" Stasia shot him a puzzled look.

"Hyde doesn't work tonight."

Aimee met his gaze with a strange look on her face, like there was something she wanted to say, but just shrugged. "Who knows?"

Stasia looked at the time on her cell phone. "I actually *do* have to get to work." She smiled at Shane. It was weak but still wonderful to see. "You wanna come by in a while? We can look over a couple of books."

"Yeah, okay." He smiled back, and it was like a cloud lifting from his mind. Stasia could always make him feel that way, even when things were at their worst. "Want me to walk you over?"

"It's across the street, Shane. I think I can make it." She winked at him to take any possible sting out of her words and stood up. "Besides, this meal's on you." She leaned over and kissed him on his forehead, then was on her way, slinging her work bag—clothes and a few books, plus her notepad for trying to puzzle out the mysteries—over her shoulder.

"Wait, I'm paying?" He frowned.

"You are? Thanks!" Stasia laughed softly and then went out the door.

Aimee stood up and shook her head, clearly distracted.

"What's up, Aimee?"

His sister looked back at him, her lower lip set out in what might look like a pout to others but what he knew was just a sign of her ruminating on something.

"I gotta talk to somebody. I'll be home later," she said. She was already three blocks down the road in her own mind, so Shane let her body try to catch up.

Which left him alone with the bill.

CHAPTER EIGHT

AIMEE HAD TO talk to Hyde.

In the midst of all the horror of the past few days, with Burroughs's murder and the monstrosity that had killed him still wandering around and then what had happened to Derek, Hyde had been doing a great job of avoiding her. Aimee had had other things on her mind, but all through the chaos the question had nagged at her. She wanted to know what was going on in Hyde's thick skull.

It had been a kiss; that was all.

Maybe.

She wanted it to be more.

Maybe.

She wasn't going to go all weepy-eyed if he shot her down. She just wasn't. It wasn't what she did. She could find other guys. But damn him, now that things had calmed down a little bit and even with the shroud of fear and grief that had fallen upon the town, Hyde was in her head all the time. She was getting tired of waiting for him to come to her. She had to do this quickly, too, because the sun was going to go down soon and her dad would have a cow if she wasn't home when night fell. That was one of his new rules, and until whatever he and Shane had seen in the cemetery was gone, that rule was going to be enforced.

Aimee walked fast, but she didn't catch up with Steve and Mark until they were at Hyde's house. She stopped just on the other side of the house next door and caught her breath, thinking about how to handle the conversation.

What if he's still fixated on Kimmie? Of course he's still fixated. He's been obsessing for, like, a couple of years. Why would that change? Why am I doing this again? We don't even have anything in common except for monsters. He's not even remotely my type. There are plenty of guys that would be with me if I wanted them. So why am I even thinking about Mark Hyde? Why can't I get him out of my head?

"Okay, forget it. Just get it done." She marched herself past the neighbor's house and into Hyde's front yard. He and Jekyll were standing near the front door. Jekyll had both of his hands in his coat pockets. Hyde was standing with his arms crossed, looking more like a brick wall than a person.

"Mark. We need to talk." She shot a look at Jekyll to let him know that now was most definitely not the time for any smart-ass comments.

Jekyll looked at her for all of half a second and then looked back at Hyde. "You know, I think I left my car in your bedroom. I'm just gonna go in there and check to see if it's still where I parked it."

Hyde scowled at Steve as he walked into the house and closed the door. Then Mark turned to Aimee and just stood there, his arms crossed and that brooding look on his face. He was the one who'd run off after they'd kissed, and it was pretty clear he wasn't comfortable talking about it.

Tough.

"Why did you take off on me the other night?"

"You caught me a little off guard, Aimee. I had to think. I just . . . didn't know what to make of it, really."

"And? That was days ago." She knew she sounded exasperated, but that was the way she handled pressure.

Hyde looked at her again, his brown eyes searching hers for something and maybe finding it, maybe not. She couldn't tell, because he almost never gave up anything.

Finally he answered her. "Look. It's a little weird for me, okay?"

"What's weird? Me?"

"No. Not you. You're beautiful, Aimee. And more than that. You're a smart girl, and you don't let anyone mess with you. I like that. A lot. So it isn't you.

But you have to understand—I'm not used to this sort of thing."

He was looking very uncomfortable, which was fine with her because she was still feeling that way herself.

"Don't talk in riddles, Mark."

He sighed. "You obviously get hit on, Aimee. You and Stasia both. Even Shane and Steve get girls flirting with them, but not me. Most people don't even acknowledge me except to get the hell out of my way."

"You're a good-looking guy."

He chuckled. "Oh, I'm not the ugliest thing walking. I've dated a few girls. Just no one from Sleepy Hollow. I'm not really well liked around here."

"Yeah, I know, class bully. The human wrecking ball. I got that part already." She shrugged. "But Mark? I'm not *from* around here."

He nodded. "I know. Believe me, I know. When you kissed me the other day, Aimee, I didn't know what to think. I mean, you know how I feel about Kimmie, and you and me, we haven't exactly had the most peaceful relationship so far." He smiled. "I'm not saying I hated the idea, by the way. I couldn't have been any more surprised. But whatever it was that was going on between us that night . . . it was pretty incredible."

Aimee grinned. "Yeah? I kinda was thinking it was just me being an idiot."

"No." He shook his head. "No way. Are you kidding? You're . . . That was . . . Just no, all right? I'm not good at talking, really. Obviously. But you're something. Truly. And if you were feeling half of what I was feeling—man, it was like being electrocuted, but, y'know, in a good way."

They both laughed, but then Aimee's smile faded and she regarded him with utter seriousness. "I was. Feeling that."

Hyde nodded. He bit his lower lip. "The thing is, I don't know if this is something I could pursue, even with the way that felt."

"Why not?"

"Well, you're Shane's sister. That isn't really very cool of me."

Aimee stared long and hard at him, but her mind was reeling back as surely as if he'd hauled off and slapped her.

"You're kidding me." She barely spoke above a whisper.

Hyde looked at her and then looked away as she started to let the words sink in. He was afraid of dating her because of what Shane might say. Just perfect. Shane was dating her best friend and now Mark Hyde, the guy she liked for reasons she still didn't quite understand, was using her own argument against her.

Irony sucked.

"You know what? I think I did something really stupid. I have to go now." She shook her head and backed away from him. "I have to go." She didn't wait any longer because if she did, she was either going to say something she'd regret later or she was going to cry, and she didn't want to do either of those things.

Aimee headed for the woods. He called out after her, but she didn't even slow down.

The crowd had finally filtered into the auditorium to take their seats, and Stasia smiled at Shane as she pulled out her books. Except for those who wandered back out for extra popcorn and soda, she had the next ninety minutes or so free.

"I thought they'd never leave," Shane said, arching an eyebrow playfully.

"Down, boy. Study time."

"Hey, I can dream," he said with a sigh.

Stasia reached out and messed up his hair. "Later. Right now we have to behave."

"What are we looking for again?"

"Anything on one-eyed giants and, of course, any references to Acephelos," Stasia reminded him. They needed to know what was killing people, and they also needed to know what the Horseman was really up to. He hadn't shown up again all of a sudden by coincidence; they'd both agreed on that.

"Too bad you couldn't bring all of your books to the theater," Shane said.

"Definitely. But I brought the ones most likely to give us something useful."

They spent about forty minutes lost in their research, interrupted only by the occasional customer who came out from the movie to get something from the concession stand. As Stasia was finishing up with a portly man who wanted an extra-large popcorn "drowning in butter" and an extra-large Diet Coke, she glanced over to see Shane gesturing toward her, pointing to the book open on the counter in front of him.

Stasia waited for the customer to go back into the theater before she went over to Shane. "Did you find something?"

"Listen to this one. We've got a thing about the Fear Lord Acephaelus, spelled differently, but we've seen that before, right?" She nodded, and he continued. "It says here that he was summoned by a guy named Lugh Lamfada to do battle with a giant called Balor."

Shane paused and read for a second, his mouth trying to wrap around a few of the Celtic names. "These guys have really got to learn what the word *phonetic* means. Anyway, he was summoned to do battle with the king of the Fomorians. That's Balor."

He looked up at her, gaze intense. "And it says

here that Balor had only one eye."

Stasia moved closer and started reading with him but had to stop when a kid came out to buy Junior Mints. By the time she got back, Shane was cross-referencing with another article in the same book.

"Okay. Listen. According to this, 'Balor of the One Eye' could kill a person with a single glance, or cause them great misfortune, or turn them to stone, depending on which description you want to follow. He was the king of the Fomorians, who were a savage race of beings that ate the flesh of their fallen enemies."

He flipped a few more pages and then started reading again. "Okay, so, Lugh was the grandson of Balor and was prophesied to bring about his death. He became one of the Tuatha de Danaan, the pantheon of Irish gods, and summoned . . . Ah, here we go. . . . He summoned Headless Acephaelus, a demon that could not be hurt by Balor, as he could not meet the Fomorian's stare. So Acephaelus is Acephelos, the Headless Horseman. Except way back when, he was just Acephaelus, and he was called to fight Balor because he couldn't *see*. The story says he mortally wounded the Fomorian king."

Stasia leaned in closer again, starting to get that excited feeling in her stomach that always seized her when they found out something important. She put her arm around Shane's waist as he continued.

"The Fomorians were made from the 'flesh of the earth' and ate their enemies. They were defeated by Acephaelus and driven away from the land, but according to this they took Balor's bones with them when they left, believing that he would come back someday."

He grunted and scrunched up his face as he looked at another of the fine-printed footnotes at the bottom of the page. "Stasia, I love your books, but did anyone back then ever just write articles to summarize what they found out?"

"No. I think it was against the law to make it easy to read or something. I haven't found one of those books that just tells the whole story at once."

"Maybe it was how they avoided getting their books burned for heresy or something." He flipped the pages again, carefully because the paper was old and yellowed.

"Okay. Let's see. The Fomorians were driven into the sea by Acephaelus and took Balor's bones with them. It says Balor will return, but his revival will be preceded by the return of the Fomorians. That doesn't make sense."

The doors to the theater opened, and the people started spilling out. Stasia stayed busy for almost half an hour, and Shane joined her in cleaning up the mess that the customers had left behind.

It was almost time to close for the night, and that was a good thing in her eyes. There was a lot of ground to cover, and she had the feeling that despite the calm of the afternoon and evening, they would need to find out as much as they could about Balor before it was all said and done.

Hyde cursed under his breath and ran to the door of his house, trying to keep his eyes on Aimee's back as she headed off into the woods. He pushed open the door and bellowed, "Steve! Aimee's bugging out. We have to catch up with her!"

Jekyll was out the door in seconds. "What did you say to her, dude?"

"I told her how I felt."

"No wonder she's running." But even as he said it, he was right next to Hyde and they were moving into the woods. The sun was setting, and no one in their right minds was going to be out in the woods right now after sunset. Something out there was killing people and maybe even driving them crazy, and that was on top of the freaky pumpkin things that kept running around and terrorizing anyone going to the wrong places at night.

Hyde spotted Aimee a few seconds later. "There she is. Aimee! Wait up!"

She just went faster, shaking her head and moving between the trees like a ghost on speed. Hyde grunted and started sprinting. Steve was behind him, not moving as quickly but probably nowhere near as winded from the run.

The girl was infuriating. Bad enough he was having trouble thinking clearly about her since the other night in her kitchen, but now she was pulling this crap. Okay, so he'd been pretty blunt with her, but she hadn't even tried to talk to him about his concerns about Shane's reaction if they got together. After what had happened with her and Shane and Stasia, Mark had figured Aimee would understand his hesitation.

He'd thought wrong.

Jekyll caught up with him. "Just kiss her already and get it over with, you moose."

"Mind your own business." He pushed ahead again and cupped his hands around his mouth to amplify his already-booming voice. "Aimee! Wait for us!"

But Aimee was gone. It was like she'd never been there at all. Jekyll and Hyde were still looking for her when they heard the cackling laughter echoing off the trees.

The noises were unsettling, but, as with most things in his life that confused or alarmed him, Hyde's reaction was to get annoyed and then to get angry.

A moment later they heard Aimee scream. This time Hyde felt something different. He felt fear.

● ● ●

Aimee hadn't lived in Sleepy Hollow that long, but she had thought she knew this part of the woods well enough to find her way home from Hyde's house. But she was pissed off at herself and at Mark and feeling hurt and embarrassed, and so perhaps she hadn't been paying close enough attention to where she was going. Whatever the cause, she had gotten turned around and now didn't have a clue where she was.

And the sun was going down. It might not be full-on nighttime outside the woods, but in the midst of the trees, it could have been midnight.

Good one. Really smart, Aimee. What's your next trick?

The trees around her were nothing but silhouettes, tall and thick and darker than the rest of the night. When she couldn't stand trying to figure out where she was for even another minute, she squatted against the base of a tree and rested her forehead on her knees.

Stupid. Everything was falling apart around her, and she felt low enough that suddenly the idea of moving away from Sleepy Hollow didn't seem all that bad.

Aimee let her hands move into the mulch on either side of her, rustling through the dead leaves and fertile soil. The woods weren't looking any less dark and intimidating, and she figured she'd catch her breath and then get walking again. She thought she heard Hyde's voice off in the distance, but she couldn't tell for certain. If it was him calling her, he was very far away. Probably it was just her mind giving her false hope. She was sort of used to that too.

She felt something sharp buried in the dirt scrape her palm and jerked back before reaching out more carefully. Maybe it was something she could use as a weapon. When she considered what could be in the woods, she thought a nice sharp stick might be a plus.

Her fingers sought it again and found the tip of what felt like some rough-hewn spear. The wood was hard and filed to a tapering end. She had no doubt she could hurt something with the weapon. She dug a little deeper, and when she was pretty sure she'd found the center of the stick's length, she wrapped her hand around it and pulled it out of the dirt for inspection.

It wasn't a stick; it was a bone. Something had worked the edge at one end into a point just as sharp as she'd expected, and even though she wanted to throw it down, she made herself hold it. Because whatever had been making bone weapons might be closer than she wanted to think about, and she might need to have a good way to defend herself.

The thought of something like that being in the area got her moving again. Aimee had no desire to hang around and look into making friends with whatever was out here. She wasn't that desperate. Not yet.

Either her eyes had adjusted, or there was light closer than she had originally thought. She examined the bone again and then looked up. The source of the light—faint though it was—didn't seem all that far off. She moved toward it, expecting to see a few houses and maybe even a streetlight that would help her figure out where she'd managed to lose herself.

She hadn't even walked fifty yards before she realized her mistake. It wasn't a streetlight or even a porch light that she was seeing. It was a fire. Not huge, but big enough and well-maintained. That would be just her luck, to run across the only lunatic in the area or, better still, a few hunters who might mistake her for a deer.

But it wasn't hunters. This was much, much worse.

She recognized them for what they were, even with the changes they had been through. First they'd built themselves out of cornstalks and then from pumpkins. Now they had found something else to use as a source for their bodies, and whatever it was had thorns.

The trickster spirits were gathered around a fire, at least fifteen of them, and they were making weapons and trophies from whatever they had killed. Their skins were thicker now, harder, by the look of them, and covered with savage-looking barbs that would probably punch through her clothes if she let them get that close.

One of them was crouched low over the fire and using the flames to harden what looked like a thigh-bone from a pretty big animal. The weapon had a wicked point, a lot like the one on her own spear. When she looked a little closer, she saw that the same creature was wearing a necklace made of teeth. In the firelight some of the teeth gleamed with silver fillings.

Aimee started backing up carefully. The last thing she wanted to do was attract the attention of the creatures around the campfire. She took two steps before she backed right into one. The thing was upside down, crawling down the tree she'd run into—its head just above hers and pointed toward the ground—and it let out a raucous screech that she echoed with a scream.

All around her the things turned and looked in her direction.

The one in the tree reached out and grabbed a handful of her hair and she screamed again, thrashing to get away. She pulled forward and felt several strands of her hair come out at the roots. It was a small price to get away from the thing. It bared thorn-fangs and hissed like a scalded cat.

On instinct alone, Aimee shoved her weapon into the thing's face. She felt the jarring impact as the point drove into its eye socket, sinking deeper than she would have thought possible. It let out a shriek of pain and fell from the tree. She wrenched her weapon out of its eye and held it close.

All around her the screaming tricksters began to move, warily circling, and Aimee ran, shoving her way past the ones that were closest.

In an instant the things were in pursuit, chasing her, leaping and scrambling through the underbrush, their bodies blending into the background as she left the only source of light behind. She heard them coming, but the farther she moved from the fire, the less she saw them as they chased her.

They heard her scream again and moved in the direction of the sound. Hyde's pulse was slamming in his ears as he thought about Aimee getting hurt because of him. There were other sounds coming from the woods, and the noises were all too familiar to them by now.

Jekyll let out a stream of profanities under his breath. Hyde couldn't have agreed more. This was only getting worse, not better.

If she hadn't screamed again, they would have missed her completely. Aimee had tripped over a root or something and gone sprawling in the woods. Hyde called her name as they turned to where she was just getting back to her feet.

Aimee saw them and screamed, "Run!" at the top of her lungs. A moment later they saw why. The damned things were everywhere, moving through the trees and on the ground.

"Get her out of here, Steve!"

Jekyll didn't argue. He grabbed hold of Aimee's arm and ran, leading her back the way they had come. Hyde took up the rear, putting himself between them and the harvest demons or whatever they were.

They'd made it almost a hundred yards through the woods when one of the things dropped out of a tree and landed on Hyde's back. Thick thorns punched through his thin jacket and shirt and sank into his skin. He staggered and went to one knee, the pain shooting through him. Hyde stood back up as the thing reached around with one thorny hand and tried for his eyes. He lowered his head at the last second, and all it got was part of his scalp and a hunk of hair.

He stopped running and bent abruptly at the waist, bucking the thing off his back and into the air. It rolled as it landed, the thorns on its hide picking up debris along the way. Hyde took three seconds to remove his belt and two more to wrap the thick leather around his hand. By that time it was back up and coming for him again.

Hyde bared his teeth and slammed his leather-wrapped fist into its rough features, feeling its jaw shatter under the impact. One of its hands caught his wrist in a viselike grip and gouged into his skin. He let out a bark of pain and hit it again, throwing all of his weight into the blow. It staggered and tore its hand from his arm.

When it swung one of its barbed fists, he tried to get out of the way, and it took advantage of his hesitation and backhanded him with the other fist. He felt the trickles of blood running down his chin and went a little crazy. Parts of the creature were covered in thorns, but there were a few areas where he could still grab it and sustain only minimal damage. Hyde reached out and caught the thing's hard chin in his bare hand and then used the one protected by his belt to grip its shoulder. He twisted. The sound of its neck breaking was like a whip crack in the darkness.

It fell to the ground and stayed there, but he could see the rest of them coming. They weren't moving as fast as he'd expected, but they were still coming in large numbers and they were spreading out.

He turned and ran. This wasn't the place to make

a stand against numbers like this. He had to get to something he could use as a weapon.

Up ahead of him something massive moved along the hill, and Hyde heard a sound like when the creature's neck breaking, only a hundred times louder. When he looked up, a tree was falling toward him. He barely leaped aside in time, branches scraping at his back as the tree fell.

When he was clear, he looked up to see what had felled the oak.

Hyde froze as he stared at the bloated red eye looking down on him.

CHAPTER NINE

THEY SPENT A good ten minutes just kissing there in the theater, and it might have gone further, but Stasia had a lot more self-control than Shane seemed capable of maintaining around her. She broke it off and insisted they get back to the books. He reluctantly agreed. They were close to something, but there were pieces of the puzzle still missing.

While he kept looking in the same book, Stasia found another one to search through. "I know I saw something about the Fomorians in here. I just have to remember where."

Shane nodded and kept reading, searching for more information about what they were up against.

Stasia beat him to it. "Here. Okay, this doesn't say anything at all about the Horseman, but it says more about Balor."

She read in silence for a minute while he continued to look in the book where he'd first found mention of Balor and Acephelos. Then she nodded and tapped the page.

"The Fomorians were made of the flesh of the earth."

"Yeah, we saw that before, right?"

"Yes, but I think I know what it means now." She set the book down and looked him in the eye. "Flesh of the earth. Which would be what? I'm going to say crops. Like corn or pumpkins, for instance."

He stared at her, putting it together, and what he came up with turned his guts to ice. The tricksters, the harvest monsters they'd been dealing with, had been popping up more and more.

"Oh, damn, that can't be good."

For a second he wondered if the series of rose-bush thefts had anything to do with the creatures, and then he discarded it. Why would they want to make themselves out of flowers, after all?

Whatever they were now, the tricksters were proof that Acephelos's ancient enemy had indeed come to Sleepy Hollow. Balor had been restored to life, and now he was seeking revenge.

Shane swore softly. "This is going to get really ugly."

Alan cut into his steak and chewed slowly and deliberately. He and Ella had only been on a few dates, none of them official or anything, and he wanted to make sure he made the right impression. Eating like a rabid pit bull probably wouldn't help him win points, and according to his daughter, dogs had better table manners than he did. Once upon a time, he'd been very well-mannered. It was the workload that had changed things, as far as he was concerned. He ate when he could and worried about tasting the food later.

Ella was barely touching her food. The idea had been for him to take her out to get her mind off the horror she had seen at the cemetery. But Alan had gotten a look at the thing, and he couldn't blame her for letting it haunt her. It wasn't just the horror of having seen such a monstrosity but the knowledge that such things could exist in the world.

"You going to be all right?" He took a sip of wine, giving her time to compose her thoughts.

"I think so," she said, and then she uttered a small chuckle. "You know, weirdly enough, I can handle what I . . . Seeing that thing should've screwed me up good, but I can take that. It was horrible, all those graves disturbed, and my heart breaks for the other families who had loved ones buried there. I know I'm going to have nightmares for a while. But do you know what's so much worse?

"It's Ed. No one should have to die like that. I've known that man most of my life. Sleepy Hollow has a long history of weird events, but creepy stories are one thing. Death like that, just erasing someone from the world. That's hard to accept."

"It always is," Alan said, glancing away, his chest constricting as he thought of his wife, Isabel, and the cancer that had taken her.

"Oh, hey," Ella said, reaching out to hold his hand. "Of course you know this. Sorry, I wasn't thinking."

Alan smiled. "No worries. Time heals all wounds, right?"

Ella nodded. "But some of them leave scars."

"That's right. Some of them do. That's all right, though. You want scars as reminders sometimes. At the same time, you've got to function. Months go by, then years, and life goes on." He frowned. "Besides, there's a difference. Isabel died of something natural. What's going on here is anything but."

She shuddered. "Or maybe it's entirely natural, just not a part of the world's nature that we're used to dealing with."

"You said the town has a long history of weird events?" Alan asked, wondering if Ella knew more than just what she'd seen. The reporter in his head never quite went away.

She gave him an odd look. "Well, I meant in the old days, the Washington Irving days. He wrote about the woods near here being haunted. That was a long time ago, but now all those stories don't seem much like stories anymore."

He took another sip of wine, this time to help him compose himself.

Ella looked into his eyes and shrugged. "You're the editor of the paper—are you going to tell me you haven't been getting unusual reports?"

"Oh, I definitely get them."

"Why aren't they in the paper more often? Why didn't you report on how Ed really died when you know the truth? You know what I saw, because you saw it too."

"Well, as much as I hate to say this, I edit a lot of what comes in. I try to focus on the stories I know are important, but sometimes I leave them a little open-ended."

Walter Traeger came over to the table, a warm smile on his face. Stasia's father was a friendly man and made it a point to stop by every table in the place as far as Alan could tell. "Look at this! Two of my favorite people at the same table."

Alan stood and shook his hand. They'd met only briefly, when they were both picking up their daughters from the theater, but the man was pleasant and could certainly cook a mean steak. Alan told him as much.

"So why edit the truth?" Ella asked once Traeger had moved on to the next table.

He wondered how to answer the question without burying himself. He decided to stick with the truth. "At first it was to help out Ed. Now it's more because I see he was right about a few things."

"Like what? How can hiding the truth be a good thing for anyone?"

"Okay. First, there was the Horseman Killer, who hasn't gone away. Second, there were some unusual drownings, and now there's been a rash of attacks, supposedly by people in weird costumes, and occasional reports of a giant walking in the woods." He shrugged. "Even if people don't see what you saw in the cemetery the other day, how long do you think Sleepy Hollow is going to have a population of relatively normal people if I start reporting all of those things without doing a little creative editing first?"

"I think I get where you're going, Alan, but humor me and give me a worst-case scenario."

"Worst case: a lot of people start panicking and move out of the area, heading for greener pastures. At the same time, every freak in the tristate area decides this is the perfect town for them. I don't think having the national news agencies setting up camp in town would do anything for tourism and business in general. Think about how bad it got here when the Horseman Killer became a national sensation."

She nodded. "Okay. You've got some good

points. But that thing I saw, Alan . . . That's not just a story. People are in danger."

"No question. But you saw the story I ran. If I printed what you really saw, no one would believe it, people would laugh at you, and they'd still be in danger. But if I run a story about an enormous, possibly rabid bear coming down from the north, people are going to be careful, they're going to be on the lookout, and if they see something big and mean, they're going to run. Isn't that the outcome we want?"

After a moment she let out a long breath. "Yeah. Yeah, I guess it is. And you're right. No one would believe it without seeing it. I know I wouldn't have."

"It goes against my nature to hide the truth from people, but I've learned that sometimes the truth is just too extreme." He sighed and cut into his steak again. "That doesn't mean I have to be happy about it."

One second Hyde was fighting, and the next he was running. Aimee had thought in that moment that they might all get out of this alive. Then came the snapping sounds of the tree cracking, gunshot loud, echoing through the woods. Aimee and Jekyll both stopped and turned at the sounds.

Hyde had just stood there, watching the tree as it started to topple toward him. Aimee was in motion, Steve right beside her, and they tackled him together, driving Hyde clear of the falling tree. Aimee felt a rush of air as it timbered past them, crashing to the ground.

Hyde rolled over and stared at the fallen tree. "Son of a bitch!"

"What's wrong with you? You could have gotten yourself killed!" Aimee snapped. She wasn't sure if she should be happy that they'd saved her butt or worried about both of them getting out alive with her.

Hyde ignored her, and as he stood, he pointed into the woods, up the slope to the west.

It stood at the top of the hill, a thing over fifteen feet tall. The face was partially hidden by the darkness, but what she could see was a nightmare. Masses of what looked like scar tissue and a huge lump of flesh covered easily half of the head. Below that, a mouth big enough to swallow her whole was parted and a thick black tongue licked across bared teeth.

"What the hell is it?" Jekyll rasped, eyes wide with fear.

The giant looked away from them for a moment, and they noticed the tricksters gathering around them in the trees and on the ground. The thorny creatures moved carefully, almost silently, save for the scritch-scratch noise of thorn on branch and leaf. Aimee looked at the things as they gathered, unsettled by how many of them had bones in their hands or as part of their ornamentation. Others had bits of clothing, cotton or denim, tied to their limbs.

Trophies. They're wearing trophies.

"What do we do?" Aimee whispered.

"The only thing we can do," Hyde grunted. "Run."

"Go!" Jekyll shouted.

All three of them bolted, running again, branches whipping at them as they sprinted through the woods.

Behind them the tricksters started to laugh and a few began to chase them, but then the giant made a kind of low, moaning noise, like a foghorn, and most of the tricksters gave up coming after them and moved toward their master.

Most. A dozen or so seemed to think the idea of chasing after Aimee and her friends had a lot more appeal.

"Where are we going?" Jekyll asked, a tremor in his voice.

"How the hell should I know? Let's just get there, damn it!" Hyde growled. "I don't want these things on my ass all night!"

The damned things were getting closer. Much closer. Their feet and hands were rattling through the trees and the underbrush alike, and their voices were picking up again, that insane cackling crow laughter that made Aimee want to scream. They were coming closer, and even as she ran for all she was worth, she knew it wouldn't be enough.

And then, as close as they were, the freakish thorn monstrosities suddenly grew quiet. Even their movement through the trees quieted down to a whisper. Suddenly, they turned and fled, darting back the way they'd come.

Aimee and the guys all came to a halt when they saw the headless rider coming their way through the woods. The black steed was moving at a light trot, and the Horseman was almost casual as he moved past them. Aimee panted hard and stared, her anger growing as the entity moved closer.

"Well, it's about damned time you did something around here!"

The Headless Horseman turned toward them in the saddle. One gauntleted hand rested on his saber, and the stallion under him snorted impatiently as it came to a stop.

"I thought you were supposed to take care of crap like this! There's a twenty-foot-tall one-eyed freak over there, and it brought a whole damned army with it! You think maybe you could go do whatever it is you're supposed to be doing around here and stop it from killing everyone?"

"Christ, Aimee!" Jekyll rasped, eyes wide and voice quavering with terror. "You think pissing off a mass-murdering ghost is the best way to handle this?"

Aimee couldn't be any more terrified than she already was, though. She pointed back the way they had come, scowling at the Headless Horseman. "The giant's that way. Go kick his ass!"

Half of her expected the saber to come out of the scabbard at the demon's side and try to take her head off. It wouldn't be the first time. Her arm still ached when the weather changed; she would never forget that Acephelos had tried to kill her before.

The Horseman leaned closer to her. Acephelos placed an arm across his midriff and stiffly bowed from the waist, a gesture that he managed to make seem mocking, even without a way to convey facial expressions. Then the stallion reared and set off, cutting through the night-blackened woods at high speed, branches snapped off by its passing.

Hyde and Jekyll watched him go, and Aimee crossed her arms. Then Mark looked at her, his bloodied face breaking into a grin. "That was so cool."

Aimee was suddenly embarrassed and looked away, and at the same time she saw Hyde doing the same thing. Jekyll stood between the two of them and shook his head.

"Guys! Get over it! Get over yourselves and just figure this out, okay?" Jekyll sounded absolutely disgusted.

"What?" Hyde demanded. "What are we supposed to get over?"

"Look, I'm walking over there and risking life and limb. I'm going to have a smoke to calm my nerves. If you two are smart, you'll just go ahead and kiss and get it done with." Jekyll stomped off a short distance away and looked back the way they had come before lighting a cigarette.

Aimee looked at Hyde.

Hyde crossed his arms. "I'm not gonna kiss you because he said to, you know."

"Are you gonna *not* kiss me because he said to?" She arched an eyebrow at him and took two steps closer.

"You sure you want to risk this, Aimee? Seriously?" She'd never seen him look less certain about anything.

"Shane can take a chance with Stasia, and if you want, I can take a chance on you, okay?"

"You know I'm a mental case, right?" He almost seemed to pull in on himself. "Seriously, Aimee. I'm not normal."

"Like I am?" Two more steps and they were face-to-face, only a few inches apart. "Not sure if you noticed, Mark, but I hunt monsters in my spare time."

"Yeah. There is that." He leaned down, almost touching her lips but not quite. She leaned forward and up and closed the circuit for him. The kiss they'd shared before had been a frantic, crushing mess that had left her with bruised lips. This was far gentler. Despite his size and his brutal appearance, his lips were tentative. She was the one who did the leading.

His hands moved over her shoulders and barely touched them, but he seemed to savor the contact. She let her own hands move over his chest and up to his neck, drawing him down to meet her.

Strange, to have him so close and not be afraid of being crushed. Almost as strange as how much she wanted the kiss to go on forever. They finally broke away from each other just as Jekyll was putting out his cigarette.

Steve looked at them with a smirk on his face. "So are we all better? Can we get the hell out of here and find a way to stop these things?"

Hyde and Aimee both shot him matching glares. He nodded his understanding. "As long as we're all in agreement."

There came the sudden noise of hoofbeats, of a horse moving fast through the woods. The three of them looked at each other.

"That's a bad sign," Jekyll said softly.

"Why do you say that?" Hyde asked.

Aimee understood, though. She shook her head in frustration. "If he's taking off so fast, I'm guessing that means the one-eyed corpse giant didn't hang around for the battle. Not this time."

Hyde nodded. "Fine. It'll happen. It's going to get messy, but it'll happen, even if I have to take the thing apart bone by bone."

Aimee smiled at him. "You're something."

"Yes, yes, he is," Jekyll agreed. "Can we just go now?"

"You got it," Aimee agreed. "But we need to get hold of Shane and Stasia. See what they've found out and get together. I don't like us all being split up now." She dug into her pocket to see if her phone was still in one piece.

Jekyll nodded. "Fine, but just because those thorny freaks scattered when the exterminator rode by doesn't mean they're gonna give up on us. If they come after us, we need to be somewhere we can put up an actual fight."

"The junkyard," Hyde said. "I've got plenty there to take care of the job."

Aimee walked with them and flipped open her cell phone. Something rustled in the woods behind her, and she glanced back to see several of the tricksters moving through the trees, shadowing them. The idea troubled her. Why would the things spy on them like that? They needed to figure this out. Now that she knew where they were heading, she had to hope that Shane and Stasia had come up with something solid.

CHAPTER
TEN

SHANE RUBBED HIS eyes and yawned. Stasia stretched at her desk, rolling her neck to get the muscles to relax. They'd come back to her house to do further research. Her books were scattered all over the place, a mess that Shane knew was entirely his fault. Aimee said Stasia was always careful to put them back in exactly the same order, but he had been digging for any more information while she looked through a few of her more unusual books to see if she could find any sort of spell against Fomorians or, failing that, against plants that happened to eat people.

"I think that's about it. And the good news is, this one doesn't require anything extra special, like a slaughtered goat."

The phone rang before Shane could respond, and Stasia answered it quickly. Shane looked over his notes at the same time, doing his best to multitask his way through his studies while eavesdropping.

"Hey, Aimee. Where are you? The reception is crappy."

Stasia listened for a minute, her eyes growing wider. "That's not good. No, I mean it. You guys need to get there as fast as you can, and we will too." She listened again, nodding. "Yeah, we think the big thing's called Balor. Do not look at its face. If you look it in the eye, it can kill you or maybe even worse. Right. Just get there. Okay. We'll come as fast as we can. Be careful."

She hung up the phone and walked over to her desk, grabbing up her notes. "Get your coat. We have to get to the junkyard, now."

"What's up?"

"Aimee and the guys are being chased by Fomorians. They aren't actually trying very hard to catch them, so she thinks they're being followed so they can report to the big boss. They were almost dead meat, but the Horseman helped them out. Now the Horseman is hunting down Balor, and Hyde wants to meet at the junkyard because he has a few things there that might be useful for fighting them off."

"Why would the tricksters follow them?" Shane asked, frowning.

"Why would Balor want them followed is the question," Stasia said.

Shane blinked several times as the thought struck him. "He knows."

"Who knows what?"

He stared at her. "Balor's big and really ugly, but he thinks. He's not stupid. The Horseman's saved our asses a couple of times. Balor's got the Fomorians following Aimee and the guys because he knows the Horseman is protecting us."

Stasia shuddered. "We'd better hurry."

Shane grabbed his coat, and the two of them started walking. Stasia took a detour to the kitchen to get an industrial-sized box of kosher salt.

"Okay, so let's see what we figured out here." Shane flipped the pages of his notes, barely looking where he was going. "The Fomorians are plant people—or at least that's how they came back from the dead."

Stasia nodded. "I'm pretty sure they were flesh before, but they're coming back as plant thingies, and according to Aimee, there are a lot more of them now."

"How many more?" Shane didn't like the sound of that.

"Maybe a hundred." He liked Stasia's answer even less.

"Okay. We're screwed. Let's keep going. Balor is a giant, and that eye is some murderous magic but only if you look directly at it, so we have to make sure no one tries to stare him down."

"Not the time for jokes, Shane."

"Who's joking? I wouldn't put it past Hyde."

"Okay, good point. Go on."

"We don't know how Acephelos beat him before, but we have to hope he can do it again. I found a reference to Balor as a Fear Lord too, so maybe he and the Horseman are both the same kind of demon."

Stasia glanced at him. "I didn't know that part. Gives me the shudders. These two are like, what, cousins or something? They're from the same family?"

Shane shrugged. "Or just have the same job description. Obviously they're not that much alike. Acephelos is vicious, but there's intelligence there, real cunning, and some honor too. He's living up to his part of the deal, right? But all I could find about Balor is that he's absolutely merciless. He had his own daughter locked away to keep her from having a son, because his grandson was supposed to be the one who would do him in. Well, Lugh was his grandson and he summoned Acephelos, so we can guess how that all worked out."

"Jeez, Lugh must have wanted him dead in a bad way." Her voice drifted a bit as she speculated.

"What do you mean?" Shane looked up from his notes and over toward her voice, just in time to avoid walking into a tree in her backyard. Stasia knew all the shortcuts, so he let her lead.

"Remember? Ichabod Crane cheated: he was supposed to sacrifice himself to summon Acephelos."

Stasia crossed her arms over her chest and shivered at the idea.

Shane stopped as the ramifications hit him. "Meaning Lugh had to kill himself to summon Acephelos. You're right. Balor must be a serious contender to make a man do that."

"I think we're talking about a war here, Shane. Not just a little argument." She looked as worried as he was starting to feel.

Shane shook his head. "We can't worry about that right now. Let's take care of getting to the junkyard." He wanted her to feel better about where they were going. He wanted more than anything for Stasia to be safe and away from what was going on, but that wasn't meant to be.

"How did Acephelos stop Balor?" Stasia asked.

"Near as I can tell, there's a limit to the power of Balor's eye. He has to rest, maybe recharge, and Acephelos had to fight him and keep him busy until Balor's eye was depleted. He only has so much juice for frying people before he gets tired out," Shane explained.

"I don't think that's the best way for us to stay alive." Stasia looked back over her shoulder at him. "The Horseman is safe because he has no head, no eyes; he can't look directly at Balor. That means if we're in there fighting with him, we could be the collateral damage while they battle it out."

Shane reached out and squeezed her hand. "We'll just have to be careful, try to keep our eyes averted. So what did you learn? Anything that would help us destroy the Fomorians?"

"Not really. But I've got an angle on that. Seems plants can be possessed, and that's pretty much what's happened here. There's a spell to drive evil spirits out of plants. It's Russian, but the translation in the book is very literal, so we might get it to work."

Shane raised an eyebrow. "Who came up with a Russian spell to stop plants from being possessed?"

"According to the book, Baba Yaga."

"Is that good?"

Stasia shrugged. "She was a witch, so maybe the spell will work. But she also ate little children and raised the dead."

"Then I guess it's good we just got the spell and not the witch to cast it, huh?" Shane said with a shiver. "Nothing on stopping one-eyed giants?"

"Only spell I've heard of that works for that requires me to cut off my head," Stasia said grimly.

"I'm gonna have to veto that idea."

"It wouldn't do too much good anyway. Acephelos is already here," Stasia replied.

Shane shook his head. "And that's the good news."

All three of them were winded by the time they reached the junkyard, but Hyde didn't waste time trying to catch his breath. He moved past the office—a trailer up on cinder blocks—and crouched behind the building, pulling several bundles out from behind the cinder-block supports.

He had a variety of lethal weapons hidden there. None of it was exactly standard issue. In addition to his gremlin basher—a baseball bat covered with razor blades and barbed wire—he also pulled out a metal staff four feet long that had been sharpened to fearsome points on each end. He slid that to Jekyll, who looked at it for a few seconds before he started grinning.

Aimee watched as the guy she tended to think of as one of the nicest geeks she'd ever met started whipping the staff around his head and body. He was frighteningly good with it.

Hyde handed her two items. One was a small shield made out of metal that had been pounded thin. The other was a homemade flail, a thick wooden shaft with a chain on one end that was tipped with a spiked metal ball.

"Lot of spare time on your hands?" she asked, staring at the things in her hands.

He nodded. "A guy gets bored, he finds new hobbies. Never can tell what's around the corner these days. So when the nasties started to show up, I did a little work in my spare time, found all the parts right here. I wouldn't go flaunting that outside the junkyard, though."

"Ya think?" Aimee tried the shield. It was small enough to fit her arm. It also felt like it could take some damage. "So, what's next, guys?"

Hyde carefully put on a padded shirt and his gloves. "I need a little protection to avoid maiming myself with the weapon I'll be using. And now I get out the heavy artillery and you guys wait here. If you stand right along the side of the trailer, you can get a pretty good view of everything coming your way."

"Where are you going?" She tried not to sound worried, but the idea of losing one-third of their fighting force—and the biggest third at that—didn't much appeal to her.

Hyde grinned. "Got me a few big toys to play with around here. We might need them."

Jekyll cleared his throat and nodded in the direction of the mountains of debris around them. "Yeah. I'm thinking we're going to need all the help we can get."

Aimee looked out at the mounds where he was pointing. Several of the trickster spirits were climbing onto the junk and crushed autos, looking toward the trailer with keen interest. They weren't approaching yet, but it wouldn't be long before they did. There was more movement farther out. The rest of the creatures were moving forward and positioning themselves.

Aimee and Jekyll kept looking, watching as more

and more of the things came out from behind junk piles.

Aimee had assumed there were maybe a hundred of the things when she saw them in the woods. She had been wrong.

They were being overrun.

"Okay, so this is looking bad. Really, really bad." Shane looked around the junkyard. Fomorians were scattered as far as he could see, taking shelter behind debris and climbing over whatever they needed to in order to get a better view. He also saw his sister and Steve Delisle holding a couple of weapons and looking completely unprepared for the growing army of monsters surrounding them.

"We have to get in there, Shane. We can't just leave them alone like that."

"Yeah, but I'm trying to figure out how we can get to them without being the main course for some of those things."

"We have to sneak in." She gnawed her bottom lip as she looked around.

Shane didn't like the sound of that but couldn't think of any other course of action. The only bright side was that Hyde, Aimee, and Steve had played it smart, leading the tricksters out here. At least out here in the middle of nowhere they wouldn't have to worry about innocent bystanders getting killed.

That didn't make the idea of sneaking past the things crawling like ants on the garbage heaps of the junkyard any more appealing.

They moved as quickly and quietly as they could to the corrugated steel fence that surrounded most of the Sleepy Hollow Reclamation Center. They managed to locate a spot where the sheet metal had been damaged enough to allow them footholds. Shane gave Stasia a boost over the top of the fence and waited for her to get out of the way before he started climbing. He sat perched on the edge of the fence for a moment, trying to orient himself before he finally dropped down into the oil and muck on the inside of the yard.

There was no light worth noticing, only the night and the darker areas where the refuse from thousands of people's lives was scraped together in a sprawling chaos. The little light that shone into the area glistened off steel and glass, leaving a halfhearted star field of debris as the only real illumination.

They moved carefully, trying to avoid making more noise than was absolutely necessary. Stasia found Shane's hand and linked her fingers with his own. He was grateful for the simple contact. It made him feel less like screaming and running away.

Off to the left he looked up at one of the stacks of rusted-out cars that had already been mashed flat and then mounded together. One of the creatures sat in perfect profile, and Shane finally understood the reason for the rosebush thefts. The creature was covered in wicked-looking thorns. They ran along its spine and covered its shoulders and head with a thick mane of sharpened points. Anyone foolish enough to hit one of the Fomorians without a weapon was going to be in for an unpleasant surprise.

Stasia moved with the grace of a cat. Shane felt like he was walking on eggshells in comparison. Every time he settled his foot down, something crunched or crumpled under his tread. Every nerve in his body seemed to stretch tightly as he waited for one of the barbed demons to notice them.

The sound came softly at first, a light tapping that seemed to come from everywhere at once. He looked around until he realized the sound was coming from the Fomorians. Those that were armed—half of them had spears or clubs of some kind—were lifting their weapons and letting the ends strike whatever it was they crouched on. They started building a rhythm: three taps followed by a soft cawing noise in the backs of their throats. Stasia's fingers locked more tightly with his own as the sound escalated in volume, building from a whisper to a pounding beat. Yet the creatures did nothing. They seemed to be waiting for a signal that had, fortunately, not come.

The sound thundered around them and Shane and Stasia started moving faster, as if to escape the racket. That wasn't possible, however, as the beasts were everywhere.

The maze of the junkyard had a certain pattern to it, but Shane didn't know it well enough to guess where they might be. They raced around a sharp corner in the labyrinth of metal, and one of the Fomorians came out of nowhere. The thing was at eye level, hunkered down on a flattened piece of plywood and beating a long bone spear against the makeshift platform in perfect tempo with its counterparts.

It looked directly into Shane's eyes and then into Stasia's, a wolfish grin straining across its face, but never broke the rhythm they were all laying out. Shane realized in that moment that they hadn't managed to sneak in at all. The creatures knew exactly where they were. They just didn't seem to think he and Stasia were a significant threat.

He started to run, pulling Stasia along with him, and she kept up easily, her face etched with fear. The cawing laughter grew louder, and the tempo of the Fomorians' odd ritualistic beat grew more frantic. For a moment he had a hope that the police were on their way, brought by the ruckus, but then he remembered that there weren't any houses for at least a quarter mile. There wasn't anyone to be disturbed by the noise.

Shane had never thought a sound could be that unsettling, that terrifying. The pulse kept building until he thought his skull would implode from the noise, and still he and Stasia ran, trying to get to Aimee and Jekyll. Still the creatures lined above them on their perches kept up the increasingly faster and louder tapping and cackling, all the while looking down on the two of them as they ran.

They finally broke into the clearing where the office trailer sat and found their friends back to back, trying to look everywhere at once as the Fomorians kept up their ritual. There was no sign of Hyde, and Shane didn't even let himself consider the thought that his friend might already be dead at the hands of the demons surrounding them.

All at once the pounding stopped.

Silence.

Every one of the thorn-hided beasts froze and turned to look back in the direction from which Shane and Stasia had come. And in the very spot where the two of them had been moments ago, looking down into the junkyard, Shane saw the giant, Balor of the One Eye.

Balor had continued to grow. The king of the Fomorians towered a full twenty-five feet in height, taller than most of the stacks or ruined cars and rubble that made up the interior of the reclamation center. His body was no longer misshapen but instead had filled out, broadened, and become complete. Thick, powerfully muscled legs supported a frame

three times the breadth of a man's, and heavily muscled arms flexed at the giant's sides. His disgusting
facial features were, unbelievably, even more monstrous than before.

Aimee and Jekyll ran over to join Shane and
Stasia, and the four of them could only stare at the
mountainous thing as it started coming their way.

"Oh, shit," Jekyll whispered.

"You're the master of understatement," Stasia
whispered, her voice hollow and raspy with fear.

It took Balor four strides to reach the fence at
the edge of the junkyard. Then he just kept coming,
slowly, inexorably, knocking the corrugated steel barrier down and crushing it underfoot as he moved
into the area where his followers awaited him.

Shane, Aimee, and their friends were frozen in
terror. Shane didn't know what to say. They couldn't
very well run now.

"This is too much," Jekyll muttered. "This isn't
gremlins, dude. We're dead."

"None of that crap, Steve," Stasia snapped coldly.
"We fight. Whatever you do, don't look at Balor's
face or at his eye. If you can't see his eye, he can't kill
you."

"Are you sure about that?" Aimee's voice was
shaking with anxiety.

"No. But we think so."

"Okay, just checking."

"Yeah, no eye, fine," Jekyll said. "But what if he just decides to break us into kindling with his freaking hands?"

"Try to avoid that," Shane replied.

"Good advice. Thanks, Egon."

"Look," Stasia said. "This guy came to the Hollow to get revenge on the Horseman. They're ancient enemies, right? So we just have to stay alive until the Horseman shows."

"And what if he doesn't show?" Aimee asked.

Stasia didn't have a reply for that.

Balor stopped well before he reached the trailer and lifted his arms toward the stars, his hands balled into gigantic fists. The sound that came from deep within the giant's chest seemed to rattle the bones in Shane's body.

All around them the Fomorians listened raptly until the noise ceased. Then the creatures dropped from their perches amid the scrap metal heaps and moved with unsettling grace and speed toward Shane and his friends.

The time had come for war.

CHAPTER
ELEVEN

HYDE DID HIS best to ignore the incredible clamor of the tricksters. If he was going to fight that one-eyed monster he had seen in the woods, he had to work quickly. The bulldozer was a monster in its own right, a beast with a gigantic front blade and several tons of mass and treads. He cranked the engine at the same time that the giant lifted its arms and started roaring. It was blind luck that the noise of the cyclopean horror was louder than the sound of the dozer starting.

He shifted gears with practiced ease. He might not own a car, and he didn't have a driver's license, but he'd been running the bulldozer on weekends for a few years now, and he knew how to make it dance.

The first wave of the things was coming down from their places among the garbage heaps and running toward Aimee and all the rest. He opened the throttle on the machine and cut them off before they could reach his friends.

Jekyll watched him go past with a smile spreading on his face. A strained and nervous smile, but a smile just the same. Hyde flipped the switch that turned on the nighttime lights, bathing the twenty or so monsters in front of him in an intense white light. They tried to shield their eyes, and a few of them remembered to move out of the way. The bulldozer caught half of them in its blade, shoving them down into the dirt and then running over them, pulping their bodies into so much vine and sap and thorn. They clawed and screamed and tried to get free, but the machine was merciless.

The giant turned to face him and Hyde lowered his head, refusing to look at the thing. He'd felt just a hint of the monster's power earlier and had been paralyzed by it. He didn't want to know what would happen to him if he looked it straight in the eye.

As it turned out, he didn't have to learn.

Impossibly, the sound of hoofbeats reached him even over the roar of the dozer. The Headless Horseman had arrived. Acephelos rode up behind the giant, and horse and rider launched themselves into the air. The stallion's eyes burned like liquid fire in the dark. The Horseman brandished his sword, and it glinted in the moonlight.

Twin hooves drove into the giant's back, staggering him, and even as he flailed and tried to regain his balance, the Horseman's blade slashed across his back, leaving a dark cut to mar the monster.

Hyde didn't bother to see what was happening after that. A lot of tricksters were still in the yard, and they seemed intent on killing his friends. He turned the dozer around, carving away part of one of the mounds in the process. The metal scrap avalanched down, and Hyde saw two of the Fomorians buried in the resulting collapse.

He pulled the bulldozer through the rest of the turn, looking for more tricksters to doze under. He saw his friends. Shane was now armed with the flail Hyde had given Aimee. She had kept the shield. Jekyll and Aimee bolted to the left, heading for what Hyde knew was a larger clearing, an intersection in the maze of scrap. Dozens of the thorn monsters went after them, and he let himself smile tightly. That was good. The more the merrier.

Shane ran up to the bulldozer, dodging a couple of the things and trashing a few with the flail. Hyde idled the machine and leaned down to listen.

"Aimee and Steve are gonna play decoys! They set 'em up and you knock 'em down!" Shane shouted. Even yelling, he was hard to hear over the rumble of the bulldozer. "Me and Stasia might have a way of stopping these things."

Hyde nodded. "Then quit talking to me and get it done!"

He gunned the engine just as a group of the tricksters started toward Stasia, who was trying to climb to the roof of the trailer. They were fast learners; Hyde only crushed one of them under the treads as the rest got out of his way. But he got three more when he backed up over them as they tried a rear attack.

Hyde headed to stop the ones after Aimee and Jekyll.

Aimee ran hard and fast with Jekyll right next to her. She used the shield to knock away some of the tricksters that came at her, but one managed to latch onto her ankle, tearing her jeans and scraping flesh, drawing blood. The pain was instantaneous and electrifying. Aimee let out a yelp and tried to bash the thing with her shield, but it was too fast. Then Jekyll jabbed with his weird, double-sided steel spear and punched a hole in its face, knocking away one eye and a cheekbone. The thing backed off after that, shrieking.

They ran some more, heading for the large intersection, which was exactly where Jekyll had said it would be. The area opened up into a spot large enough to accommodate tractor trailers turning around. Most of the debris around them was now from automobiles, not just standard junk. Cubes that had once been cars were stacked all around them in treacherous-looking piles. And not far from those, the junkers still awaiting their date with the crusher were sandwiched one atop the next.

The stacks were all covered with the things Shane had called Fomorians. There really wasn't any time left to panic, which was a weird sensation. She wanted to freak out but didn't dare. So instead she put all her strength into slamming the small shield on her arm into the face of one of the tricksters. It let out a cawing battle cry and tried to tear the shield away from her arm, the barbed fingers of the thing seeking to clutch the metal and wrest it away.

Aimee kicked it in the kneecap and shattered the joint. At the same time, Jekyll whipped that stick of his around in an arc and slapped three of the things across their heads.

The bulldozer came around the corner, several of the things clinging to it and trying to get at Hyde through the metal framework that surrounded him. He used his baseball bat to punch one of them on the arm and lost a few razors from his weapon. That was all right. The Fomorian lost an arm in exchange.

Hyde pushed the bulldozer into a higher gear, and it lurched forward. A couple of the tricksters hanging on lost their balance and fell free. One of them got hooked into the treads of the machine and shrieked and wailed as it was dragged under.

Aimee didn't have time to think about that.

Instead she let out a scream as one of them pulled her shield from her arm and threw it away, hissing and smiling at her. Aimee looked around and found a good place to grab hold of the stack of cars next to her. She scrambled like a monkey, using climbing muscles she'd stopped employing around the age of nine. They came after her, moving with disgusting ease and making her wish she'd never stopped taking gymnastics. One of them grabbed her foot and started pulling. She had two choices: lose the sneaker or fall back into the growing tide of the things. One second the trickster was starting to tug down on her and the next it was looking at her pink sock and the Reebok in its hand. She found a thornless spot on its forehead and kicked it in the head, then watched it fall back off the perch it had managed to secure.

Aimee finally managed to reach the top of Car Mountain, warm blood sticky on her ankle. Heart pounding, she turned just in time to see Balor sweep one massive arm out—so much faster than she would've expected—and knock the Horseman out of the saddle. The horse crashed over onto its side with a crack of bone and a hollow sort of thump. The Horseman spun through the air and struck the ground in a tumble, sword flashing. Acephelos was a demon of extraordinary power. He did not lose his grip on his blade.

Horse and rider both rose almost instantly. The Horseman whipped his blade through the air and leaped twenty feet into the air to land atop another tower of debris. The Fomorians perched up there wailed and backed away, terrified.

The massive black charger kicked at several of the tricksters, breaking them open as its hooves slashed and stomped. One of the demons landed on the horse's back and attacked, digging its claws deep into the animal. Aimee heard the horse scream and then it rolled over, crushing the creature under its own weight and righting itself in only a moment. Not an ordinary horse at all. Not even close.

The roar of the bulldozer became suddenly louder, and then the car pile she stood on shifted under her. Aimee screamed, trying to keep her balance, and looked down to see that Hyde had slammed the stack with the bulldozer's blade, crushing half a dozen tricksters against the metal.

She heard a shout from nearby and turned. Balor had been distracted from the Horseman by something a couple of rows of metal slag away from her. She saw the giant's head twist, saw its huge, bulbous, tumorlike eye open. It gleamed red and then fired a blinding beam of light that spilled out and seared metal and the ground, but she couldn't see what it had been looking at.

I can't stay here, she thought. Shane might have

just been killed—or Stasia or both—and she wouldn't know it. She had to do something.

The metal under her creaked and shuddered a second time, and Aimee let out a scream as the entire thing shifted.

"Aimee! Get your ass down here!" Hyde's voice was desperate, and she carefully looked over the side to see that he'd pushed the bulldozer up to the stack of scrap cars and raised the scooping blade so it was almost level with the top of the heap. He was standing up in the seat and looking up toward her, his baseball bat in one hand and the other holding on to the edge of the bulldozer's canopy. His face was grim and bloody.

"Can you climb onto the blade? I'll bring you down."

Several of the Fomorians were pinned under the treads, and she could see them coming for her from both sides. With no other choice, she scrambled down to the thick metal blade and settled herself across the top of it, one arm and one leg on either side.

Instead of lowering her down, Hyde sat back down and gunned the engine, pushing at the gigantic heap of cars. Aimee screamed like a banshee as the entire thing shivered and groaned and then started tipping over, sliding in a cascade.

The mountain of cars crashed over, several of the

flattened vehicles rolling into the next pile before they came to a halt. She didn't know if Hyde had meant for it to happen or not, but the stacks on either side of the one he'd knocked down collapsed as well, bringing close to twenty tons of metal down around the bulldozer.

The Fomorians tried to escape, but they were standing on the scrap piles that fell and she could see them being crushed, pulverized by the wrecks that came down around them. One of the crushed vehicles bounced off the bulldozer, pushing it two feet to the left, and Aimee bit her tongue as she clung desperately to her spot on the top of the scoop. Hyde stayed where he was for a second and then climbed half out of his seat as a thorn-covered, hag-faced trickster jumped on the canopy and tried to get to him.

Where she'd seen Balor moments before, something exploded into a fireball, and the scrap yard lit up with red light, as though hell itself were coming to earth.

Shane hurried back to Stasia's side, panting, left hand stinging from a deep cut where he had grazed one of the monsters. Stasia was busily spilling salt in a pattern on the ground and had to warn him to watch his step. Whatever ward she made would be useless if he kicked the salt into disarray.

The black horse of Acephelos ran past without its rider and charged toward the gigantic form of Balor. Big as he was, they could barely see the giant over the hills of debris that littered the entire area.

Something moved in Shane's peripheral vision, and he looked up to see Acephelos leap right over their heads, crossing a fifteen-foot gulf between towers of scrap as though it were a single step. The Headless Horseman landed in a crouch, a terrible wraith of a demon now, and for a moment his body turned as though he were glancing back at Shane and Stasia. In that moment, staring up at the stump where the demon's head should have been, Shane *felt* the Horseman's gaze upon him.

Acephelos jumped to another tower of automobile wreckage and then out into the air, dropping down into the saddle of the fire-breathing stallion. The horse paused, reared back as though to get its rider more comfortable in the saddle, and then horse and rider charged, heading back toward Balor. All around them the Fomorians scattered, terrified of the Horseman even as he merely rode past. Shane could feel the fine hairs on his neck rise as he watched. He understood their fear.

Unfortunately, they weren't anywhere near as afraid of him and Stasia, and they were coming back again. Stasia put down the salt and Shane snapped it up, filling his left hand with the stuff.

"What are you doing?"

"They have eyes, don't they? I'm gonna see about blinding a few of these things."

With the salt in his left hand and the homemade flail in his right, he waited for the tricksters to come. Stasia did her best to work through the spell, carefully reciting the words she'd written down. He thought what she was doing was having an effect because he could feel a cold chill that seemed to emanate from the salt patterns. He hoped it wasn't just his imagination.

With a terrible chorus of cackling laughter that was like claws on his spine, a cluster of the Fomorians attacked. He threw his handful of salt in a wide arc away from the pattern that Stasia had created and managed to hit most of them in their vulgar faces. In their eyes.

They roared and capered about, covering their faces. One was still coming at him, and Shane swung the flail. Thick metal spikes broke through the hard wooden skull of the thing and it dropped to the ground, injured but not dead. Had a human been struck the same way, getting up would have been impossible. But the Fomorian rose anyway, thick reddish sap flowing from the wound it had suffered. He hit it again as the rest staggered around, trying to get back their eyesight. It backhanded him on the chest, the thorns on its hand breaking off in his jacket.

Stasia finished her chant and stepped back from the salt sign she had poured. Whatever it was supposed to do, it didn't make the creatures around them any less active.

"Okay! Let's get out of here!"

"I don't know if it worked, Shane!"

"Neither do I! We can't worry about it right now." One of the things jumped at him, its face set in a mask of insane rage, one eye completely corroded by the salt he'd thrown. He flinched, unprepared for the attack. The thing hit the air in front of him and bounced as surely as if it had run into a brick wall.

More importantly, where it had hit the invisible barrier, its body smoked and slowly started to burn. The Fomorian screeched and rolled, trying to stop the pain, but it did no good. In a matter of a few moments it was blackening all over and stopped moving. The ward radiated a wave of natural power that destroyed the presence of anything supernatural.

A little ways off, something exploded, sending flaming debris into the air. The ground shuddered, and several of the heaps of garbage around them shivered as well, a stove and a rusted tractor chassis crashing to the ground.

Jekyll had meant to stay with Aimee, figured there was strength in numbers, but there were too many of the damned tricksters around him, and then she'd started climbing up one of the piles of cars and he'd found himself suddenly outnumbered.

He started moving the sharpened staff Hyde had made him in wider arcs and kicked at the things that came too close. Jekyll had taken martial arts classes from the age of seven until he'd started high school, and while he wasn't some badass, he still remembered plenty, including fighting with a bo stick, or a staff. Of course, the ones he'd trained with weren't metal and didn't have sharpened ends, but he very much liked the weapon Hyde had made.

The tricksters quickly learned to be wary of the weapon he was using and of his ability to inflict damage, but most of the ones he hit were getting back up, and that just wasn't a good thing. So Steve ran, looking for cover or at least a better position from which to fight. He saw Hyde moving the bulldozer toward Aimee and hoped they would both be okay, but this had become a matter of self-preservation.

The tricksters kept coming, making their raucous noises and moving all over the place, scrambling across obstacles that were too sharp or too slippery for him to even think of climbing.

Then one of the thorn monsters grabbed a piece of junk from the ground—he thought it was the lid from an old charcoal grill—and hurled it at his face. Steve ducked but lost his balance and fell on his side. The staff he'd been using to keep them all at bay dropped from his hand and rolled away. One of the things grabbed it and started swatting at him. Jekyll got up and backed away fast.

"Oh, come on now, this is just getting stupid."

Apparently the things didn't agree, because they started coming in faster, and the little snot that had come up with the idea of throwing things started gathering bottles and other potential missiles to hit him with.

"Screw this!" Jekyll ran hard, using his hands to keep his balance when he had to and wincing several times when he felt his skin get grazed or sliced by jagged edges.

There had to be something he could use to get rid of these things. Unfortunately, Hyde had already taken the bulldozer. Not that Jekyll knew how to drive one anyway.

A dented soup can bounced off his ear, and he smiled as he saw it. It hurt, but it also gave him an idea. Jekyll ran to his left, cutting through a couple of stacks. He didn't exactly know this place as well as Hyde, but they'd gotten stoned here a few times in the past, and he also came here to hang with his bud on days when going home after school didn't suit him. So he was pretty sure he could remember where to find what he was looking for.

He looked over his shoulder just in time to catch

a rock across his cheek and ran faster. He had to get to the bottles before they could figure out what he was doing, and he had to get them to the same spot. Getting them to follow was easy. Getting to the bottles without getting killed was going to prove harder.

He rounded a corner and collided with something the size of a tree trunk with the texture of cold, wet leather. Steve knew what it was without looking and he shuddered, unable to breathe, as fear wormed its way into every cell in his body. It was Balor. He'd run right into the giant's leg. The skin was dark and rancid, stinking of rot and death. Jekyll gagged and backed away.

Balor turned its huge eye to look upon him.

Jekyll ran faster than he had ever imagined himself capable of. He couldn't help himself . . . he glanced back and saw the thick eyelid start to rise.

The Fomorians that had been chasing him were startled when he reversed direction. Some of them dove aside and others scrabbled at the ground and tried to turn around themselves. But why hadn't they just attacked him? Then he realized it wasn't him they were trying to escape. The world around him lit up and he felt tempted—so very tempted—to turn and look. It was almost as though Balor could exert some kind of force upon his will, could make him turn around. Jekyll slowed and even began to swing around, but then he bit hard on his lower lip and the pain seared his mouth, shaking any temptation out of him.

The red light brightened with a flash like lightning, and he looked ahead and saw his own shadow cast on the ground and debris ahead.

But it didn't touch him. Didn't hurt him.

Several of the creatures around him made the mistake of looking at their king. Apparently they weren't immune to the monster's gaze. Three of them froze where they were, their eyes wide and their mouths open in a gaping scream. Four of them within the field of that sickening light caught fire instantly, and he heard others screaming but couldn't see what happened to them. He was far too busy running.

And then the light was gone and he was still alive. He tried to laugh, but no sound would come from his mouth.

The Horseman charged past him. Jekyll lunged out of the way, but the horse clipped him and knocked him off his feet. The rear hooves of the beast came within inches of crushing his head into the dirt. He lay on the ground, aching from the impact. But when it was safe to lift his head again, he saw what he'd been looking for and smiled.

Jekyll pulled off his coat and then took off his T-shirt in the cold night air. He put on his coat again as quickly as he could and then ducked as a trickster lunged at him. Jekyll gave it a side kick to stagger it and then another to knock it down. He ran for the chain-link fence before it could get up again.

Some things ended up in junkyards that were just too volatile to leave out in the open. Things like bottles. Not for soda or beer, but for propane gas and other explosive forms of fuel.

Steve scaled the fence, making no effort to hide his actions from the tricksters. He crawled in deep, sliding between stacks of mostly empty canisters, and as he went, he turned the wheels on several of the containers, opening the valves. Not all of them gave out a satisfying hiss that revealed they weren't empty, but some of them did. Enough.

The tricksters laughed madly and clambered after him like monkeys, climbing the fence and leaping over the top, thorns rasping against metal.

Jekyll finished opening as many of the bottles as he could and hoped it would be enough. Then he went to the far side of the enclosure and scrambled under the fence in a spot Hyde had shown him before, a place where local dogs sometimes found their way into the yard. The fence rattled, and the Fomorians hissed in response.

He smiled tightly as he pulled out his lighter and struck the flame. It sucked giving up one of his best Superman T-shirts for the cause, but he figured it beat getting eaten alive by the things trying to sniff him out.

The cotton-and-polyester blend smoked for a few seconds as he tried to light it and then it finally caught fire. Jekyll looked through the chain links and counted at least fifteen of the damned things in among the canisters, with more still climbing over.

He put two fingers into his mouth and blew out a sharp, piercing whistle.

The Fomorians looked his way and started calling out in their crow-speak. He threw the now-blazing T-shirt over the top of the fence and watched it drift down in a shower of smoke and sparks.

Then he ran like hell.

Seven seconds later the world behind him exploded.

CHAPTER
TWELVE

ACEPHELOS RODE BACK around again, his cloak mostly torn away and the steed under him limping.

Balor stood before him, bloodied by numerous cuts and otherwise unharmed.

The Fomorian king held a grudge and meant to see the Horseman destroyed.

To Acephelos, the giant was merely unfinished business.

The two enemies charged at each other, Balor kicking aside a half ton of garbage as he came for the Horseman. Refuse filled the air and masked the sound of the Fomorians who had been lying in wait.

They came from beneath the loose debris and rose in a wave, fifteen, perhaps twenty of the cringing demons that had run from Acephelos whenever he showed himself. They feared him, these creatures, but not as much as they feared their master.

Horse and rider went down, buried under a moving wall of thorn-covered flesh. The Horseman's saber cut fast and hard, chopping through limbs, but the demons surrounding him were too many and they held him in place.

And Balor, their king, laughed deep within his chest as he came closer.

The giant towered over him and lifted one foot, prepared to grind him into the ground.

Jekyll made it to the first of the garbage heaps and dove for cover, praying hard.

The new sun that had risen bathed the entire area in a blast of heat and light and thunder.

Jekyll looked up at the fireball as it rose, sending Fomorians and gas bottles alike through the air. One of the larger canisters must have had a decent amount of fuel left in it, because it went spinning end over end through the air, spewing a massive tongue of flame in its wake.

The canister rolled through the sky and came down onto the broad back of Balor. The impact ruptured the metal and it exploded. The giant was blasted into a mountain of discarded furniture and broken boards recently set in place after a house fire. One of the thick support beams from the remains of the house lanced through his shoulder and drove out through his back.

Balor screamed, a sound nearly as loud as the gas explosion. The giant pushed back against the heap of debris that crumbled under his weight and rose to his full height, his eye wide open and blazing its light into the sky.

Shane and Stasia watched from the safety of the circle she'd made, the ward that protected them from the tricksters. The Fomorians near that circle continued to wither and blacken and fall to the ground.

Aimee and Hyde stopped the bulldozer just as it rolled over another two Fomorians. The creatures had finally realized that they were not as powerful as the machine and most of them merely ran from it, knowing that their king would destroy the humans within it when the time came. From their vantage point Aimee and Hyde could see the agonized expression on the giant's face as he tried to pull the seven-foot spear from his chest.

The giant looked around, seeking what might have caused him such incredible pain. Shane and Stasia turned away. Hyde and Aimee would not look directly at Balor's face. Wherever his gaze fell, Fomorians died or were driven insane.

Jekyll could only cower and watch in horror.

Balor froze when he spotted Acephelos, and several of his followers were incinerated as the Horseman rose to his feet and ran for his mount. The giant started to move after him, but the enormous support post lodged deep in his body made that impossible.

More of the gas containers exploded in the distance. Balor roared again. Jekyll tried to make himself very small. The giant's great gray hands wrapped around the thick wooden post that had impaled him and Balor pulled, trying to remove the wood buried in his flesh.

In a moment he would be free.

Shane and Stasia watched the effects of the ward she'd created. It weakened as it radiated farther away from the intricate sigil she'd written with salt, but still, it was definitely working. Within a few hundred feet of them none of the creatures survived, and even those that came too close would suddenly sway and start to blacken.

They might have been able to stay perfectly safe through the entire thing, but Stasia had seen something that frightened her even more than Balor.

"We have to go, Shane. The giant was staring at something, but I couldn't see what. It might be Aimee or one of the guys. We better go check it out while Balor's still busy. I don't think he's going to be distracted for much longer."

And she was right about that. Even as she was speaking, the giant worked at pulling the stake out of his chest, and though he grunted and screamed as he did it, he was making a lot of progress. He'd pulled the wood a couple of feet out of the wound, and where it had been inside him, it dripped a thick blackish fluid. Instead of seeming weakened by the new damage, the Fomorian king seemed to be getting stronger.

"Yeah, okay. Let's go do this." Shane grabbed up the salt and handed it to her, nodding as she poured a heavy handful into her palm and closed it into a fist.

A second explosion rocked the ground and sent debris raining down around them. They tried to stay to the center of the path, and though few of the creatures seemed to have much fight in them, they were prepared for the worst. A small handful of the things came for them, staggered but still strong enough to attack.

Shane hit one with his flail and was shocked when, instead of being wounded, it completely shattered. The ward did it. It appeared to be leaving the Fomorians weakened. He wasn't about to complain.

When the next one attacked, he wasn't fast enough. The thick thorns sliced a few more pieces of his coat away and punched into his skin underneath, but not deeply. Not this time. They were definitely weaker and slower than before. Shane kicked the thing and watched it stagger back, its leg breaking when it hit a half-buried tire in the dirt path.

The other two died quickly, and Stasia finished off the one he'd started on, hitting it with a two-by-four until it stopped moving. They were no longer making sounds, save to creak weakly.

"This is weird. It can't be the ward doing this. That wouldn't work this far from where I cast it." Stasia's words mirrored his thoughts.

"Maybe the Horseman is doing something to them?"

Stasia nodded. "He has to be."

At last, with a great roar of pain and rage, Balor pulled the rest of the beam from his chest. Even as they looked, careful not to let their gazes lock on the huge, bulbous eye, they saw the wound in the giant's chest closing.

Then they heard Jekyll screaming.

As soon as Aimee was on the ground, Mark ushered her into the bulldozer's sheltered cover and they started moving again, pushing at the weakened creatures, crushing them under the treads and wrecking them with the blade. They tried to run, but even those not being hit by the machine were falling, their skin blackening in patches as they tried to escape.

"What the hell is happening to them?" Hyde sounded almost disappointed that they weren't putting up more of a fight.

"I don't know and I don't care; just keep smashing them!"

Hyde didn't have to be told twice. He started pushing through the ones that didn't get out of the way fast enough, heading for the source of the earlier explosion. Any doubt as to where it came from was removed by the second fireball that illuminated the night. In the brilliant flash there still seemed to be dozens of the Fomorians left, and they were way too active for Aimee's taste.

When she spotted a number of them running from stack to stack, she let Hyde know about them. He knocked over another of the mountains of debris, sliding alongside it and forcing the bulldozer into an angle where she thought for sure it would flip over. None of the tricksters managed to escape.

They kept moving as the fire grew larger in one corner of the junkyard, and Aimee felt her stomach knot up with dread. They were moving closer to the giant too, and even as she thought of him, Balor roared.

The giant bared his thick, jagged teeth in a roar of challenge and spun in search of Acephelos. The headless demon was nowhere to be seen, and the thought that the Horseman might have avoided his revenge was enough to enrage Balor.

Below, he saw the human that had caused him pain. He strode toward it. The human tried to hide from him, but he lifted it into his hand, savoring the fear that radiated from its filthy, sweating flesh. It wailed its terror into the night.

Even as he lifted it closer to his face, more of the vile things came forward, two in some sort of metallic wagon that blazed with lights and two more on foot. He made sure they could see the one he held in his hand, and then he raised its struggling form until it was level with his eye.

The ones in their machine charged, the thing moving toward him with sudden speed and the oddly shaped front end lifted up as if to shield them from his gaze.

Balor didn't bother looking at the passengers. He merely kicked out with his leg and let his mass do the rest. The machine rolled and spilled its passengers into the dirt. The screams of the humans that fell from within it merely added to his joy as he lifted his prey close and glared with his smaller eye.

Most could hope to survive if they were crafty enough not to look into his evil eye; Balor knew that well. He also knew that none could withstand the fury of his gaze from so close.

Balor opened his massive eye and felt the venoms that brewed within it focus, ready to eliminate the demon Acephelos's pet.

Aimee shook as she and Hyde crawled from the wreckage of the bulldozer, bashed and bruised but mercifully lucky. No bones were broken, and they been thrown clear, so they had not been crushed underneath the machine. Her pulse raced with terror. Frantic, she looked around to see Stasia and Shane running toward them. Shane pulled her to her feet, and then the ground quaked with a chilling roar. All of them looked just as the giant began to open its gigantic eye.

The light from within the giant was a presence at this range. They could feel the power that emanated from within the glowing orb, and Aimee thought of the hell poor Steve was about to experience.

She screamed in anguish, hands clutching the side of her head, crying out for some divine intervention that she knew would never come.

Hyde ran for the monster, screaming, his fists balled up and his face set in pure rage as he tried to protect his friend. He never had a chance. Balor didn't seem to even notice as Hyde lashed out with his fists, striking the giant's leg with enough strength to shatter human bones.

Aimee cried out for him to stop, but he was deafened by his desperation.

Then, from the shadows amid the piles of wreckage, the Horseman appeared. His horse lunged out of the darkness, eyes glowing and nostrils flaring with fire. The Horseman raced at Balor but reined the stallion back and reached down to grab Hyde under one arm. He raised Mark off the ground and flung him away like a rag doll.

Aimee held her breath and stared in astonishment. Mark weighed two hundred and fifty pounds, and to the Horseman he was as light as a feather.

Then the Horseman pulled the reins, and his great black beast reared up and drove its hooves into Balor's gray hide, dragging deep trenches of dead, rotting meat away.

Balor screamed and turned away from Jekyll—from the prey in his hands—to focus on his ancient enemy, even as Acephelos and his stallion attacked again.

With Balor distracted, the Horseman made his move, leaping from the back of the hellish horse. His cloak, tattered and ruined, spread like black wings, illuminated by the junkyard fire, and Acephelos leaped into the air, his saber aimed directly at Balor's blazing, venom-filled eye.

The strike was true and the vile eye exploded, spewing scalding hot fluids across the ground. Where the liquid touched, the very ground blackened, and metal hissed, slagging into a puddle of ruin.

Balor reared back, the Horseman holding on, riding the giant, thrusting the blade deeper. The giant dropped Jekyll from his hand, a forgotten toy, lost in his sudden agony.

Jekyll fell toward the ground and Hyde, just standing up, tried to catch him and half succeeded. The impact was too great, and both of them hit the soil only inches from the venomous puddle. Neither moved.

Above them the Horseman withdrew his saber and then slashed again and again, carving a gaping hole where moments before Balor's eye had blazed. The giant staggered, fell backward away from the group, and landed hard, his body knocking still more debris aside as it came crashing to the ground. The great limbs thrashed for only a moment and then were still.

For one moment silence reigned, and then everyone tried speaking at once. Aimee ran to Hyde and Jekyll, with Shane and Stasia right behind her. She checked on Hyde first and felt his neck, looking for a pulse. At the same time, Shane grabbed Jekyll and pulled his still form away from the seething black fluids.

Stasia helped Aimee drag Hyde, both of them straining to move his body at all. Just the few seconds in which they'd breathed the air above the boiling blackness had been enough to make them weak.

And as they struggled, the Horseman climbed down from the body of Balor, patches of his clothing blackened and burnt.

Behind him, the gray body of the Fomorian

king began to crumble as if made from little more than ash.

Acephelos turned in their direction for a moment and sheathed his blade. Then he made a formal bow that almost seemed directed at Aimee and moved to where his horse waited.

He leaped onto the stallion's back and spurred the horse on, galloping hard away.

Jekyll and Hyde both moaned and Jekyll coughed, his face set in an expression of pain. Hyde rose to his knees and looked back at the remains of Balor, which were falling into little more than powder.

Of the Fomorians, there was no sign. Most of the tricksters had been killed, burned, or crushed or withered away. If some had survived and run, there was nothing the Lancasters and their friends could do about it.

Ten minutes later they heard the sirens and started away, each of them bruised and bleeding but alive and safe.

EPILOGUE

ALAN LANCASTER WAS the one who found them. The station wagon pulled to the side of the road that led to Hyde's house. Somehow he knew that was where they would go.

He'd tried calling home a dozen times and had felt his heart freeze in his chest when the first of the explosions rocked the neighborhoods within hearing range.

Later he would tell his children that most of Sleepy Hollow was in range of the noise. But for now he merely pulled over and climbed from the inside of his car, looking at the five teenagers with awe.

None of them were willing to talk just then, and despite his need to know all that happened, Alan just ushered them into the car and drove them to his home. There would be time for talking later, after the fires had been extinguished and after he'd concocted some fiction to explain the chaos for the

Gazette. It seemed wrong that the people in the town would never know what this quintet of kids—most of whom were looked upon with suspicion and even disdain by so many in the Hollow—had done for them.

But that would all wait. For now all he cared about was his children and their friends. He was a father first, after all.

For tonight the people of the Hollow would simply have to make up their own lies while they hid behind closed doors and clung to their fear. They were safe, but they didn't know that.

Still, it would keep.

Just for tonight, it would keep.

ACKNOWLEDGMENTS

Chris would like to thank Liesa Abrams and Margaret Wright for their invaluable contributions, Ford Gilmore for his faith and constant enthusiasm, Connie and the kids for the love and hugs, and the usual suspects, Tom, Bob, Amber, Jose & Lisa, Rick, Ashleigh, Tim, Wendy, and all the V.C. guys.

Ford would like to thank Chris for being such a great collaborator and an ideal creative partner; my mother, Tomm Coker, Susana Santiago, Kyle Carpenter, John Byers, Brendan McGuigan, Ben Vanaman, and Michael Slain for their support and being good sounding boards; and Washington Irving for the inspiration.